TOO CLOSE FOR COMFORT

ADAM CROFT IS A BRITISH AUTHOR, PRINCIPALLY OF crime fiction, best known for the Kempston Hardwick mysteries and Knight & Culverhouse thrillers.

His work has won him critical acclaim as well as three Amazon bestsellers, with his Kempston Hardwick mystery books being adapted as audio plays starring some of the biggest names in British TV.

His books have been bought and enjoyed all over the world, and have topped a number of booksellers' sales charts. Adam is also a regular contributor to BBC radio discussions on broadcasting and mental health issues and has been a columnist for the Huffington Post.

Also by Adam Croft

The Kempston Hardwick Mysteries
EXIT STAGE LEFT
THE WESTERLEA HOUSE MYSTERY
DEATH UNDER THE SUN
THE THIRTEENTH ROOM

Knight & Culverhouse
GUILTY AS SIN

Non-fiction works
WE NEED TO TALK ABOUT ADAM
TIPS FOR WRITERS

Too
Close For
Comfort

Adam Croft

Notes for the New Edition

Independent publishing has come on a long way since I first published my first book, *Too Close for Comfort*, in January 2011. My only intention for the book was to put it online so that one or two strangers could read it and let me know what they thought of it. Because of this, it wasn't the most highly-polished thing I've ever written and I've never really been happy with it. But hey, it was out there.

The next thing I knew, it had topped the Amazon bestseller chart and sold 80,000 copies and counting. Whoops. My priority then had to be in developing both the Knight & Culverhouse series and my other main series, the Kempston Hardwick Mysteries, and a number of other projects which brings me to now, March 2014. Put simply, it was time to revise *Too Close for Comfort*.

The book has been revised and embellished, some details changed, to better suit my writing style and incorporate everything I've learnt over the past three years, as has the second book in the series, *Guilty as Sin*. It will also help tie in with the continuation of the Knight & Culverhouse series, in which new books will be released in the coming months.

I hope you enjoy the new edition.

Adam Croft

1

DS Wendy Knight stared at the crime-scene photograph of Ella Barrington. Ella's swollen purple face looked lifeless as her head sat indented in the mud. Blood had trickled from her nose and dried onto her lips. Her eyes had the appearance of glass, almost doll-like.

It wasn't how Wendy had expected to spend her morning, but she had waited to be called onto her first murder case for a long time. DCI Jack Culverhouse, in his usual inimitable style, was giving a run-down to the rest of the investigation team.

'Ella Barrington, aged twenty-one. Prostitute.'

Wendy smiled to herself and gave a small shake of the head. Culverhouse's reputation preceded him: he always got to the important details first.

'Discovered by an early commuter at Mildenheath Train Station at six-thirty this morning. We've got a combination of strangulation and suffocation, according to the SOCO boys. Oh, and her throat was slashed, too. We've no way of telling yet what actually killed her, but I think we can rule out a tragic accident.'

A nervous chuckle rippled through the incident room.

'All forensics can say at this stage is that it's almost certain she died on the spot where they found her — there's mud under her fingernails which matches indentations in the ground, and it doesn't look like she was dragged there after she'd died. Her throat was cut, but they reckon that was done after she'd died.'

'Which direction?' Wendy asked.

'Sorry?'

'Which direction was her throat cut in? You said they knew.'

'From left to right, apparently, but I don't see what difference it makes at this stage, Knight.'

Wendy knew that one could tell a lot from the direction of a cut. 'It makes quite a bit of difference, actually. It makes him right-handed.'

'What?' Culverhouse asked, seemingly put out that someone so new to murder investigations should have the audacity to show him up like that.

'You said her throat was cut from left to right. That means the killer must have been right-handed.'

'Listen to me, Knight. I've not got time to listen to your theories on bloody forensics — that's why we've got those dickheads in white suits crawling all over the body.'

'I was only saying—'

Culverhouse shot a telling stare in Wendy's direction. That was her cue to shut up and listen.

'The body was easily identifiable. She's known to most of the response units, and let's just say the desk sergeants have had to deal with her a fair few times. Besides which, she had her driving license on her in her purse, which made identification somewhat easier.'

'She still had her purse on her?' Wendy asked.

'Correct. Any more bright theories you'd like to enlighten us with, Knight? Apart from the bleedin' obvious, I mean.'

Wendy thought twice before saying anything.

'That means the killer wasn't motivated by money or stealing her possessions,' Culverhouse said. 'Our motive wasn't theft. Boys and girls, we're looking at a cold-blooded prossie killer.'

Wendy was amazed that Culverhouse had ever managed to scale his way up the apparently politically-correct modern police force. She recalled a story she had been told by a colleague when she mentioned that she was looking to join CID. Legend had it that Culverhouse's wife had done the dirty on him and run off with his child, leaving him with a deep hatred of women. She had heard that he would go out of his way to make sure that prostitutes and female petty offenders would be dealt with swiftly and to the fullest extent of the law, even if it meant the odd con getting away with murder — sometimes literally. Of course, she also knew that the working environment of the modern police service meant that rumours and supposition were rife.

There was an air of intrigue around the SIO; there was no denying that. Wendy, though, had always been wary of DCI Jack Culverhouse and his hard-cut reputation. Now, on her first real murder case, she knew she was going to need all the help she could get. Talk about being thrown in at the deep end.

Debbie Weston, a middle-aged Detective Constable who'd was also relatively new to CID, whispered to Wendy, her blonde hair arced over her eye as she tilted her head. 'I really don't know how he stays so calm and jokey. I'd be bricking it if I had to lead a murder investigation.'

'It's a case of having to, Constable Weston. Murders are simply business. You can't let it get personal or it'll eat away at you until there's nothing left,' Culverhouse barked. Debbie Weston was a new addition to the department and would have to learn the hard way about Culverhouse's legendary supersonic hearing. She got the impression that he spoke with a voice of experience.

The ringing phone pierced through the hubbub in the incident room. DS Frank Vine leaned across the desk and answered it.

'It's for you, guv.'

DCI Culverhouse strode confidently towards the desk and listened to the voice on the other end of the line for a few seconds.

'Same MO?'

He sighed, before murmuring a 'thank you', replacing the handset and turning back to the now-silent incident room.

'They've found a second victim.'

2

TERROR AND EXCITEMENT SURGED THROUGH WENDY'S body. Ever since she was a young child, Wendy had longed to work in CID and revelled in solving murder mystery books and television programmes long before the end of the story. Every budding detective dreamed of their first serial-killer case, but there was absolutely no way she could have ever prepared for the brutal reality and sheer panic she felt right now.

The surge of terror sank to the pit of Wendy's stomach, giving her little warning as she vomited violently into the toilet basin. The relentless deluge stopped her from even catching her breath, as if desperately trying to expunge the terror and anxiety from within her.

Wendy had always assumed she would follow in her father's footsteps. She recalled overhearing her dad telling her mum about the people he'd locked up that day. *Street cleaning*, he called it. Of course, that lack of confidentiality would result in disciplinary action today, but Wendy's father came from a different world.

There were words she didn't know at the time: rape, prostitute, dismemberment, mutilation. But as she grew older and learnt to fill in the gaps, it served only to further fuel her desire for justice and the sense of awe and excitement at the thrill of the chase.

She remembered seeing her dad's ID card sat on the hall table after he returned from the station each night. She had never told him, but she used to creep downstairs every evening and polish it with her nightie. She chuckled to herself now as she recalled it.

Wendy always escaped to the dream world of her childhood under times of stress. It was a safe haven where there were no criminals, no rapists and no murderers. If there were bad people, her father would have dealt with them; she had no fear on that front. Now, her father wasn't there to pick up the pieces. Not only that, but the person tasked with dealing with those problems was her.

Before long, reality had set in again and Wendy longed to be back in her dream world. The thought of these young lives being ended so horrifically had her retching into the toilet again.

As she returned to the incident room, Culverhouse was ready and waiting like a creature ready to pounce on its prey. The animalistic similarities did not go unnoticed by Wendy.

'Nice of you to join us, Knight. I've had Weston all round the fucking station looking for you.'

'Sorry, guv. Nature called.' The mere mention of nature had Wendy smirking at the creature stood before her.

'There's nothing funny about your fucking bowel movements, Detective Sergeant Knight,' he boomed in an embarrassingly loud voice. 'We've got a double murder investigation on our hands and you're part of this team. Next time you want to bugger off and sit on the bog for twenty minutes, you ask me. All right?' Wendy felt firmly put in her place.

'Right,' Culverhouse continued. 'Now we need to get moving on this one. DS Wing and DS Vine — I want you onto the MO. Explore the connections between the two murders. SOCO seem to think there are some, but we need to know more. Knight, you're coming to the Common with me. We're going to view the scene before forensics get their grubby mitts all over it. Weston and Baxter, you're coming too.'

Wendy raised an eyebrow. Luke Baxter was barely out of his two-year probationary period, let alone an officer with any sort of CID experience whatsoever. To Wendy, he was little more than a work-experience boy. A black rat who had wormed his way into a suit for the cachet. Why on earth was Culverhouse taking an inexperienced woolly-back to a murder scene? To what looked like a serial murder scene at that. She had had the misfortune of working with Baxter before, outside of CID, and knew what a slimy git he could really be. She thought twice about commenting and realised she had nothing to lose.

'Baxter's coming?'

'Yes, Knight, he is. Do we have a problem with that?'

'Not at all, guv. I just thought maybe there was some paperwork he could be getting on with here. We're getting snowed under already.'

Shit. She'd only spent a few hours in the company of Culverhouse and already she was turning into a bigot.

'Baxter's going to be a part of this team, Knight. He's going places and he needs to experience certain things. You catch my drift?'

Wendy's mind wandered to a time when she had first seen a dead body not long after joining the police force, when she was still on the response team in her probationary period. A woman beaten to death by her husband. She could vividly recall her thoughts and feelings as she first entered that living room.

It was the smell that had hit her first. That foul, rotten stench seared through your nostrils and stayed with you for the rest of your life, hiding somewhere deep within and pouncing in your least guarded moments. Dreams were a particular favourite moment for the beast to pounce. She remembered seeing the body lying on the floor in a mishmash of colours. The blonde hair, the brown dried blood, the blue skin. Oh god, that blue, lifeless skin. The sight and smell had made her sick then, too.

Wendy never ceased to be amazed at how a dead body could look so different to a sleeping, living person. It was as if with the passing of life, a light had gone out somewhere. In the absence of any other credible evidence, this gave Wendy her spiritual belief. If we are simply bags of bones and blood, Wendy thought, how can there be such a distinct lack of soul and being in the empty shell of a dead person? As humans, we instinctively know someone is dead just by looking at them. She knew there had to be a reason behind this.

Wendy hated murder scenes. Just because she'd never had to work on a murder investigation itself, she had attended her fair share of suspicious deaths. Although she tried to appear nonchalant every time, inside she was a quivering wreck. Now it was Baxter's turn. That slimy, goody two-shoes had been nurtured and fathered by Culverhouse ever since he joined the force. Butter wouldn't melt in Baxter's mouth as far as Culverhouse was concerned.

Yeah, let him experience it. Let him see it. *Let him see it, the bastard.*

3

THE GRASS ON MILDENHEATH COMMON WAS A YELLOW-ing colour. The scorching summer had been particularly unkind to it that year, with the inevitable hosepipe ban having come into force in mid-July.

As they crossed the grassy area from the gravel car park to the crime scene, Wendy couldn't help but smirk at the horror that Luke Baxter was about to experience. The warm weather would make the smell even worse, even if the death was fairly recent. The putrefaction would usually begin a few hours after death, with the organisms in the digestive tract multiplying and producing gases and odours. In this weather, though, that'd happen even quicker. During particularly hot periods, an adult human could become a skeleton in two to four weeks.

Upon reaching the body, the foul, pungent smell hit Wendy like a ten-tonne truck, and Luke Baxter even worse.

'You all right, Luke?' Wendy asked innocently.

Wendy could see Baxter's face turning a pale shade of green before her very eyes.

'Yeah, fine. Just a bit… you know. The weather and that. Bit pongy.'

'I'm sure you'll be fine.'

The body lay lifeless on the ground, just as Ella Barrington's had. Her body had started to swell — a sure sign that putrefaction was well under way, and her face was crawling with maggots.

'He's had a right good go at her, guv,' a man in a white suit said.

Wendy never ceased to be amazed at the specialist talent of some of the SOCO boys — stating the bleeding obvious.

'We can see that. What have we got?' Culverhouse asked.

'You'd be better off asking what we haven't got. She's been suffocated, strangled, and her throat has been slashed. Sound familiar? Someone wanted this woman dead, and they weren't going to mess about with it.'

'What else do we have?'

'Well we're pretty sure that it's the same guy who did Ella Barrington, if you ask me. Which, of course, you didn't. There are a number of patterns that link the two. I'd go out on a limb to say they're definitely linked.'

'Fantastic. You always know how to brighten my day, you SOCO lot. Tell me more about these patterns.'

'Well, there's still a lot we need to look at. I can tell you that the killer was almost definitely right-handed.'

'What makes you say that?'

'See these slash marks? You can see the entry point of the knife and the way the pressure has been applied. We can tell from the knots, too, on the ropes tied to her wrists and ankles. They were almost definitely tied by a right-handed person.'

Wendy shot a wry smirk in Culverhouse's direction. It was met by a faint, but definite grudging nod of acceptance.

'You noting this down, Baxter?' Culverhouse asked.

No answer. Culverhouse spun around to where Luke Baxter had been standing. He was gone.

'Fucking hell, that's all we need. Did anyone see him move?'

'Nothing, guv. He was stood behind us all, so he could be anywhere.'

'You're really helping, Knight. You're really fucking helping,' Culverhouse said.

The officers split into three groups and spread across the common to look for Luke, while two SOCOs stayed at the crime scene. Wendy and Culverhouse were in a pair, and headed toward the wooded area at the edge of the common.

'Permission to say I told you so, guv?'

Culverhouse's silence told Wendy everything she needed to know. As they approached the edge of the common, Culverhouse began to call out. Wendy could sense exasperation in his voice. Or was it desperation?

'Baxter? *BAXTER!*'

Luke Baxter came jogging out of the copse in front of them.

'Yeah? What is it, guv?'

'Where the fuck have you been? We've got a sodding search party out for you!'

'Sorry, guv. I, uh, wanted to explore the wider area a bit more. Get a feel for the crime scene, you know.'

Culverhouse's eyes moved towards the vomit stain on Baxter's jacket.

'Got a feel of this morning's breakfast at the same time, did you?' he asked.

Wendy was delighting inside as Baxter's face turned an impressive shade of red.

As they returned to the body, Culverhouse continued his conversation with the SOCO.

'Right. Where were we?'

'The interesting thing, Jack, is that the killer has made no attempt to conceal either this young lady's body, nor that of Ella Barrington. As you can see, we're wide out in the middle of the common. We'd usually expect to find a body buried or at least hidden in the undergrowth. It's almost as if he wanted her to be found.'

'He?' Wendy asked.

'Oh, yes. We're almost certainly looking at a man. The brutality of the struggle is evident and, with the greatest respect, there's no way a woman tied knots like these.'

'Do we have a positive ID yet?' said Culverhouse.

'Yep, she still had her bag and purse on her. It doesn't seem as though your man made any attempt to steal anything. She's Maria Preston. One of your men said she was a well-known local prostitute.'

'We'll end up with a shortage if we're not careful.' A ripple of nervous laughter followed Culverhouse's remark. 'Right, well it looks as though we've got our biggest link yet. Two murders, two prostitutes. Any more theories, Knight?'

4

THAT EVENING, AS WENDY MADE HER WAY TO HER BROTH-
er's flat, she couldn't help but play the same line over and
over in her head.

It's almost as if he wanted her to be found.

Why on earth would the killer want his victims to be
found so easily? Why would he not want their flesh to
decay, their bodies to rot so badly that the police could
not identify them as easily as they otherwise could? Did
he want the police to find him just as easily? The questions
kept encircling Wendy's mind.

She thought back to her own personal studies into murderers and serial killers. The Green River Killer, who was
thought to have killed more than fifty people in Seattle,
Washington, in the early 1980s left his victims in the open

on the banks of the Green River. Again, all women and mostly prostitutes. He was never caught. Lucien Staniak, the Red Spider, who killed eleven women in Poland in the 1960s used to write letters to the police telling them where the bodies were. For some killers, it was all part of the game.

Michael's flat was situated in a less than desirable part of Mildenheath, to say the least. The flats just off of Wiseman Road were fairly new, but still pretty drab and depressing. The Hillside estate was pretty depressing in itself, and recent "regeneration" efforts had not done much to improve its local reputation. Wendy knew, through her job, just how much of the local crime originated on the Hillside estate. It wasn't the sort of place her brother should be, but at the stage in his life he was at, he didn't really have much choice.

As Wendy drove through the dark, dimly lit streets, she recalled the last time she'd visited Michael's flat. Cigarette ash was sprinkled all over the sodden furniture and a mixture of blood, semen and sweat had worked its way into the filthy carpets. Wendy shuddered as she anticipated the scene she would witness this time.

She parked her car in a well-lit corner of the communal car park and made her way up the metal staircase that scaled the front wall of the building.

As Michael opened the door and she entered the flat, Wendy felt an overwhelming sense of sorrow. The siblings that had shared parents, shared a household, shared a childhood. How could they grow up to be such entirely different people?

'It's good to see you again, Wend,' Michael said as he closed the door behind them.

'And you, too. How are you bearing up?'

'Yeah, pretty good actually. That's why I called you over. I'm starting to pick myself up. As you can see, I'm already getting the flat in order.'

Wendy looked around at the muck and filth that consisted of Michael's home. Cobwebs adorned every crevice and mould was almost visibly crawling up the walls.

'Yeah, so I see. It looks... great.'

'Coffee?'

'Uh, no, I'm fine thanks. I can't drink coffee too late in the evening,' Wendy lied. Drinking coffee in the evening was almost a habit for her. It had to be, if you were more often than not up all night poring over case notes.

'Oh, right. Well I'm afraid I don't really have anything else to offer you. I've not been to the shops yet this week.'

Wendy hoped the sigh of relief wasn't made out loud.

'And the drugs?' Wendy asked. 'Have you stopped the drugs?'

Michael had been a heavy user of both heroin and crack cocaine and had made life very difficult for Wendy in recent years. As the only family member he had left, she felt almost responsible for him. Even though she wasn't, trying to work your way up through the police service and having a drug addict and petty criminal for a brother wasn't exactly ideal. Work and family life don't mix well at the best of times, but the previous few years had been particularly awkward.

Michael smiled and made his way through to the kitchen to pour himself a coffee.

'Course I have. Been clean a few months now.'

Had it really been that long since she had last seen Michael? It must have been. She had rarely felt compelled to pay him social visits in the previous years, knowing that it was both a waste of time and a possible conflict of interests. Although Michael's criminality had long been a thing of the past, she hadn't got round to visiting him for some time. The days had turned into weeks and the weeks into months.

Out of the corner of her eye, Wendy noticed something: a syringe containing a small amount of brown liquid adorned the french dresser in the living room. Even without her narcotics training, it was pretty evident that the needle was used and had once held heroin.

She said nothing and waited until Michael returned with his coffee.

'A few months, yeah? Then what's this?'

'That? Oh, that's from a friend of mine. He's homeless but comes here occasionally to score. He's not managed to kick the habit yet. I really should stop him coming over, I know. It's not a good influence.'

Wendy may only have seen Michael a handful of times in the previous few years, but she still knew when he was lying.

'Tell me the truth, Michael. This is yours, isn't it?'

'It's not as easy as you think, Wend. I'm trying... I'm trying.'

'Trying? *Trying?* Haven't you learnt anything, Michael? Dad would turn in his grave if he knew you were pumping this shit into your arms. Or have you started on your legs yet?'

'I'm trying! I swear to God I'm trying! Do you have any idea how hard it is to just stop after seven years? I've been doing this fucking shit for seven years, Wend. It's powerful stuff. It's not as easy as that. The methadone dulls some of it, but it's not the same.'

'Don't give me that bullshit, Michael. You're not even interested in trying! Even through mum's illness you carried on pumping that shit into yourself without a care in the world.'

Michael seemed visibly wounded by the mention of their mother. Sue Knight had died three years earlier from pancreatic cancer, mentally scarred by having to watch her only son slowly kill himself with class-A drugs. The initial shock of her death had seemed to jolt Michael back into reality, but grief had soon set in and he dealt with it the only way he knew how. Since then, they'd barely spoken.

'It was the only way I knew how to cope.'

'Cope?! Don't make me laugh! It was probably you and your addiction that finished her off!'

No sooner had Wendy uttered those words than she had immediately regretted every single one of them.

'Wend, I called you because I need you. I need help.'

'You've had my help whenever you wanted it for the past seven years, but nothing's changed. Nothing will ever change. How many chances can you give someone? I'm through with you, Michael. I don't want anything to do with you,' she said through breaking tears.

Whether through anger or guilt, Wendy left Michael's flat, slammed the door behind her and headed for her car.

As she coasted through the streets of Mildenheath, Wendy played the conversation over and over in her head. She could recall every word, every inflection. It was something she seemed to make a habit of, although she wasn't quite sure whether it was the mark of a good police officer or a character trait that left her unable to forgive and forget.

Stopping at the traffic lights on Southold Street, Wendy's eyes drifted over to the pub, The Cardinal, at the side of the road. Swinging her car round to the left, she pulled into the car park and walked into the pub.

She pulled up a stool and perused the drinks on offer, her eyes stopping at the bottle of whisky attached to the optic. She didn't even like whisky, but right at that moment it had an appeal.

'Whisky, please,' she said to the barman, a middle-aged bloke who looked like a rat.

'Heavy day, was it?' the barman replied.

'You could say that. Can you make it a double?' She'd leave the car in the car park, she decided. The walk home would probably sober her up anyway, and she could do with the thinking time.

The barman duly obliged and collected the money from his new friend for the evening. Despite being a town centre pub, The Cardinal never seemed to get much passing trade. It once had a reputation as a rough pub, and the exterior decor did it no favours in lifting that reputation, the blue paint peeling and flaking off the door and window frames.

'Penny for 'em,' the barman said.

'You wouldn't want to know, trust me.'

'Copper, are ya?'

'How'd you know?'

'We get a lot of them in here. Easy to spot, really.'

Wendy wondered whether they ever got a lot of anything in The Cardinal. She certainly saw no reason for any of her colleagues to drink in a dive like this. Except Culverhouse. She'd bet Culverhouse would love this place.

'It's a long story.'

'Try me.'

Wendy thought for a moment. She could be careful, not give away too much information. 'OK. Yes, I'm a copper. I'm attached to a murder case which is now a serial murder case. There's a nutter on the loose who's chopping down prostitutes, and we're miles from catching him because my senior investigating officer is a clueless bigoted prick. For a brief respite, I went to visit my idiot smack-head brother this evening only to find out that he's still an idiot and still a smack-head. How's that for starters?'

'Better than most I hear, I'll give you that. First I've heard of any serial killer, though.'

'We've only just found out ourselves. It's due to hit the papers in the morning. Will be on the front page of tomorrow night's Bugle. Call it a sneak preview.'

'I'm honoured. You nowhere near catching the fella then?'

'Not really. There are still a few things to tie up.'

Wendy guffawed at the terrible pun and realised she needed another whisky.

The barman rang the bell for no-one's benefit but Wendy's. Christ, it was half-eleven. She didn't know what time she'd arrived at The Cardinal, but it was a good four double whiskys ago. With no other option, Wendy said her goodbyes and left.

The walk wasn't an option at eleven-thirty. All she wanted to do was go to bed. She didn't think twice about getting into her car and driving home, even after her good four whiskys. Tonight, she just didn't care. In fact, the thought rather amused her.

As she reversed her Mazda out of the parking space, she realised she hadn't switched on her lights. As she fumbled to do so, she looked up and into her rear-view mirror just in time to see the large four-wheel-drive BMW meet the rear bumper with an almighty bang.

Wendy got out of her car and apologised profusely to the man in the BMW, who'd got out and was inspecting the damage.

'Shit, I'm so sorry. I didn't see you there. Are you OK?' Wendy asked.

'Yeah, I'm fine. Car's a bit worse for wear, though. Christ knows how you managed that – I wasn't even moving!'

'I'm so sorry. My mind was elsewhere and I just went onto autopilot.'

'It happens. Just as long as you're insured, mind!'

'Don't worry about that. I can go one better: I'm a police officer.'

'Well, saves me a phone call, I suppose. You on licensing, then?'

'No, night off. I'm attached to the murder squad, actually. Wendy Knight,' she said, proffering her hand.

'Blimey, a real professional woman. There's a turn-up for the books. I'm Robert, by the way. Robert Ludford, seeing as we're onto surnames already.'

The man handed Wendy his business card in a manner far too unsuitable for the occasion.

Robert Ludford ~ Chartered Accountant.

'Blimey, a real professional man, too. There's a turn-up for the books.'

The pair chuckled as they exchanged insurance details before heading back to their cars.

'Oh, and Wendy?' Robert called. 'Be careful, won't you? Whisky and cars are never a good mix. You wouldn't want to have to arrest yourself for drink-driving.'

5

WENDY STAGGERED INTO THE INCIDENT ROOM ON TUESday morning with the most horrendous hangover. She was sure she had only had four whiskys, but it felt like forty. One of the many pleasures of getting old, she concluded.

'Christ, Knight. You look like the back end of a horse.'

Wendy admired Culverhouse's unique concept of a compliment.

'Thanks, guv. You don't look so bad yourself,' she replied, clearing a pile of papers from her desk and propping her backside up on it. She cradled her cup of coffee, the steam rising up her nostrils.

'Heavy night, was it?'

'No, I just went to see my brother.'

'Didn't realise smack gave you a hangover.'

Wendy shot a loathsome glance towards Culverhouse, who visibly stepped backward and raised his hands, as if in mock defeat.

'Well, it's nice of you to join us, anyway.,' Culverhouse said. 'We've had Steve and Frank getting to the bottom of the MOs and there are a number of matches.'

Wendy was willing to bet money that the only thing Detective Sergeants Steve Wing and Frank Vine had been getting to the bottom of were a succession of *McDonald's* bags.

'Firstly, both our victims were prostitutes. It might seem a little cliché, but I think this is probably the route he's going down. There's no evidence so far that the women knew each other, at least not from what their families and friends have told us, but we're sure it's the same guy who finished them both off. Too many patterns.'

'What patterns?' Wendy asked.

'Well, each of the victims was found with a length of rope tied around their necks. The rope used for each victim was different; Ella Barrington's was a manila hemp whilst Maria Preston's was a blue plastic sort of rope. The weirdest bit is the way they were tied. Now, I'm no expert, but they weren't your usual knots. Frank was in the boy scouts when he was younger, and he reckons they were — what did you say they were called, Frank?'

'Bowline knots, guv. Pretty handy for nooses.'

A shiver ran down Wendy's spine as she quizzed DS Vine for more information.

'But he didn't hang them, did he? I mean, why tie a noose if you're not going to hang them?'

'Nah, they weren't hanged. There's no sign of broken necks or any kind of blunt trauma from the rope. You see, the bowline knot is often used for situations where the knot will come under a lot of strain. It's not the most common one for your average serial killer to use; it's quite a specialist knot, you see, mainly used by sailors and anyone who has ever been in the boy scouts. The interesting thing is the amount of mud that had been collected in the fibres of the ropes. It would lead me to think that he'd tied the rope around the girls' necks and dragged them to their final resting places.'

'Shit,' Wendy said.

'Yeah, but that's not what happened. The bodies them-selves had shown no sign of being dragged anywhere. The mud around them wasn't disturbed in that way. You wouldn't drag a live body, anyway. For all its strengths, the bowline knot is very easy to untie. Besides, the mud embedded in the ropes was too localised. If they'd been kicking and screaming, much more of the rope would have come into contact with the mud than we're seeing here.'

'So what are you saying? That the rope was used for something else first?' Wendy asked.

'Possibly. We're getting the mud checked, but we're pretty sure it's the same stuff as at the common, which doesn't help us much. The other possibility is that Ella Barrington and Maria Preston weren't his first victims.'

'Shit. What about the cause of death?'

'The throat-cutting, most likely. It seems as though the whole noose idea was some sort of perverted game; they were probably already dead at this point, as there aren't any rope fibres under the victims' fingernails.'

Just as Frank had finished talking, Steve Wing turned up the volume on the television. It was a local news report on the murders.

'*— but the Police have not said whether they believe the two girls were connected in any way. What they have said, however, is that they believe the killer may strike again and urge women in the area of Mildenheath to take extra care when leaving their homes.*'

As the camera cut back to the studio, Culverhouse was distinctly unimpressed.

'Nice one, Steve. Next time maybe you can let us see the other ninety-five percent of it.'

The tense atmosphere was cut short with a rap at the door of the incident room.

'DCI Culverhouse? I'm Patrick Sharp,' the man said as he entered clutching a manilla folder full of papers.

'Sorry?'

'The psychological profiler. I presume Chief Constable Hawes told you I was coming?'

'I'm afraid our esteemed Chief Constable has a habit of telling me fuck all, Mr Sharp. Do come in.'

As Culverhouse took a seat next to Wendy, Patrick Sharp perched himself on the edge of Culverhouse's desk and proceeded to address the team.

'Well, it seems as though we've got precious little time to waste, so I'll get straight into it. Despite immediate appearances, the personality of the man we're looking for is quite common amongst serial killers. The fact that he seems to leave his victims in rather findable places signals that he is trying to initiate a sort of game with the police. He's very methodical, too. The cuts to the throat and the tying of the knots were remarkably neat, and the similarities between the two murders are striking. He strikes me as a very orderly man — obsessive, some might say. The peculiar knots point to some military training, perhaps.'

Culverhouse had the look of a grandmother being taught to suck eggs.

'However, the information I have at this time is very brief. I believe SOCO intend to provide me with some more information shortly, so I'll have more for you then.'

And with that, Mr Sharp stood up and left the room.

'Well that was fucking useful,' Culverhouse said. 'I could have told you that myself.'

As the officers returned to their respective desks, many heads shaking, Wendy's phone rang.

'DS Knight?' she said as she held the phone between her head and shoulder.

'Ah, Wendy. Hello – it's Robert, Robert Ludford.'

Wendy paused whilst she tried to match a face to the name through whisky-clouded thoughts.

'From last night? Surely you remember, Wendy.'

'Oh yes, sorry. I'm still rather tired. How did you get my work number?'

'You gave me your card.'

"Did I? Sorry, it's all a bit of a blur. What can I do for you?'

'Well, it's more of a case of what I can do for you, actually. I was wondering if you might like to come out for dinner one night. I know a fantastic restaurant in Walverston.'

Whisky-clouded thoughts of the impending murder investigation and her argument with Michael were not helping Wendy's mood.

'No, I don't think that would be very appropriate. Sorry, Robert. Goodbye.'

No sooner than Wendy had hung up the phone, it rang again.

'*What?*' she barked, now getting rather annoyed at Robert Ludford's odd behaviour.

'Oh, hello. Is that the incident room for the Mildenheath murders?'

'Yes, sorry,' Wendy said, straightening herself up. 'Who am I speaking to?'

'My name's Mrs Connors. Alma Connors. I think I know who committed these terrible killings. I think it was my son.'

6

Alma Connors's house smelt faintly of cats. As the sweet old lady guided Wendy and Culverhouse into her living room, Wendy noted that her son must be in his forties by now. Either that, or Alma Connors was a very late starter.

The house was a smell red-brick mid-terrace house on Elizabeth Street, not far from the town centre, in the Royals part of town, built in the early 1900s.

'Can I get either of you a cup of tea?' she said as she ushered Wendy and Culverhouse into her living room.

Culverhouse quickly surveyed the scene, noting the cat smell and the bird droppings on the mantelpiece before curtly answering for both himself and Wendy.

'No thank you, Mrs Connors. That's very kind of you.'

'Well, I suppose I should get straight to the point, then.'

Culverhouse wished very much that she would. He wasn't particularly good with smells.

'As I mentioned to DS Knight on the telephone, I believe my son may be the man you are looking for in connection with the recent killings.'

'Right. And what makes you think that, Mrs Connors?'

'Call it a mother's intuition, if you will.'

At this, Wendy cast her eyes towards Culverhouse, knowing exactly the look she would find upon his face.

'Mrs Connors. As much as it pains me to say it, intuition does not go down very well as admissible evidence in court. Now, if your "intuition" is the only reason for calling me and DS Knight away from a very important investigation, I would like to warn you that it could very well be considered as wasting police time."

'Oh no, Inspector. There's plenty of evidence, believe you me.'

Culverhouse had a feeling that Alma Connors's definition of "evidence" may differ slightly from his.

'You see — my son, Thomas, or Tom, as he likes to be called, was dating a young lady up until recently. Quite a nice, young lady. Very polite. However, it was quite clear, to me at least, that she wasn't your usual run-of-the-mill girlfriend.'

Culverhouse's patience was running thin. 'Go on, Mrs Connors.'

'Well, she was… You know… A lady of the night.'

'You mean she was a prostitute?' Wendy said.

'Yes, if you like. Now Thomas has never had many girlfriends, so I think it was all rather convenient for him. He suffers from some social difficulties, you see. Asperger's Syndrome. I'm quite sure the relationship never became sexual. Not under my roof, anyway. He used to buy her all sorts of nice gifts with the money he had saved and I think he just quite liked having a young lady friend to feel proud of.'

'And how does this tie in with our investigation, Mrs Connors?' Culverhouse asked.

'Well, if I remember correctly, he stopped bringing this girl home a couple of weeks ago now. I asked him what had happened and why she didn't come over any more and he acted very evasively. He wouldn't even mention her name any more, Inspector. To go from borderline infatuation to complete ignorance in an instant struck me as rather queer.'

'Rather queer indeed. But I must ask you *again*, Mrs Connors; how does this tie in with our investigation?'

'Well, I was watching the news reports on the killings and they showed a picture of each of the young girls. I'm almost certain that the second one was Thomas's young girlfriend. Maria Preston. I think that was her name.'

'You *think* it was her name?' Culverhouse said.

'Well, yes. That's not what Thomas told me she was called. He said her name was Lauren, but I suppose these ladies of the night must operate under all sorts of false names and secret identities.' Alma Connors seemed nervous and uneasy at the situation which had presented itself to her, yet strangely keen to tell all.

'Yes, I suppose so.'

'I really didn't want to have to do this, Inspector. It's a terrible thing to have to report your own son to the police, but after seeing what happened to those young girls, well, I had no other choice.'

'And you're quite sure it's Maria Preston that Tom was seeing?'

'Quite sure, Inspector, yes.'

Culverhouse had already opened his mouth to ask Alma Connors another question when the living-room door opened. A man in his late thirties entered the room gingerly and rather nervously. Wendy supposed the man would not look out of place at a comic book convention.

Alma Connors looked rather shocked at the man's sudden entrance.

'Inspector Culverhouse, this is Thomas, my son. Sit down, Thomas.'

'Inspector?' Tom Connors asked nervously.

'Detective Chief Inspector, actually. This is my colleague, Detective Sergeant Wendy Knight. Pleased to meet you, Tom.'

'What's this all about?'

'We'd like to ask you a few questions about a girl you might know. Known to you as Lauren, I believe.'

Tom Connors looked visibly distressed. 'What about her?'

Culverhouse, not wanting to alarm Tom Connors, chose his words very carefully.

'We believe she may have been involved in accident.'

'I don't have anything to say about her.'

'It's not quite as simple as that, Tom. This is a criminal investigation and if we believe you may have some information which could help us, then we do need to talk to you.'

'I told you. I don't have anything to say about her.'

'Tom, if it turns out that you did know this woman then you don't have much choice. We'd like to you accompany us to the police station so we can have a little chat.'

'Oh, will that be necessary?' Mrs Connors said. 'Only it's best that Thomas can stick to a routine, and to places he knows.'

'Mrs Connors,' Culverhouse said, as calmly as he could manage, 'if what we've been speaking about turns out to be of some significance, we need to do this properly.'

'Don't worry,' Wendy added, hoping to placate her. 'We'll make sure he's comfortable with everything.'

As they left Alma Connors' house, Wendy gasped at the fresh, cat-free air that flowed outside. She couldn't have been more pleased that Culverhouse had decided to conduct the questioning at the station. Tom, clearly uneasy and well out of his comfort zone, put up quite a resistance to Culverhouse's insistence that the conversation be continued elsewhere. A quick, sharp jab to the ribs (thankfully unnoticed by Wendy or Alma Connors) soon sorted that out.

As the unmarked Vauxhall pulled away from the house, Wendy's mobile phone rang. The conversation was brief, and she had soon put the phone back in her jacket pocket.

'That was Mildenheath Hospital,' she said numbly. 'Drop me back at the station and I'll drive over there. My brother's been taken ill.'

'Ill?'

'Drugs overdose, they reckon. They've asked me to come in right away.'

7

As Wendy drove through the congested town centre of Mildenheath between the police station and the hospital, a torrent of mixed feelings flowed through her.

Although one part of her felt no sympathy for Michael — she despised drug abusers — she could not help but remember that he was her brother, after all. She knew all too well through her job that anyone could make mistakes. Right now, she was determined not to let mistakes get in the way of what they had as siblings.

The memories flooded back: visions of them riding their bikes around the cul-de-sac they'd grown up in, sitting on the grass verges playing with dandelions and making beds out of grass clippings. Mildenheath had seemed a much safer place back then. It had still had its traditional market town feel, long since lost to the traffic jams and exhaust fumes of the faceless town centre full of empty shops.

Wendy sighed inwardly at the number of charity shops and takeaways which seemed to comprise the only trading businesses in the town. She sat waiting in the right-hand lane at the traffic lights in the town centre and could sense the driver of the next car staring at her. Unable to ignore the feeling, she glanced to her left. The man looked dishevelled, yet Wendy got the sense that he somehow knew something. Even at this distance she could see the piercing blue eyes of his expressionless, yet all-knowing, face. This town was full of some odd sorts.

She tried to imagine the state Michael must be in. She envisaged wires and tubes coming out of his mouth, a machine beeping at his bedside. The pang of guilt was unbearable as she recalled their argument the previous night. Had it made Michael take an overdose? Had she caused this? *No*, she told herself. She couldn't feel responsible for Michael's problems. They were his responsibility and his only, and the sooner he recognised that the sooner he could get back to where he needed to be. Where he should be.

Wendy glanced back towards the car next to her. He was looking at her again. As a child, Wendy often wondered if people in the street could read her thoughts or somehow know what she was thinking. As she sat in her car, those thoughts came flooding back. Did he know something?

The whys and hows of Michael's condition seemed somewhat irrelevant. Since her mother had died, Wendy was the only person Michael had. The realisation didn't make her feel any better about the fact that she had barely seen him since.

Despite the green light, the traffic was not moving. An accident further up the road, Wendy presumed.

As she rolled her head back onto the headrest, Wendy closed her eyes. She tried to blot out the bad thoughts by recalling more of the better days with Michael, when both were young children, playing happily in the back garden of their family home. As she sat at the top of the wooden slide, she could feel her father's large, strong hands on her sides. He let go, and she slid down the slide and onto the lawn. The slide had once been varnished but was then beginning to splinter. Wendy supposed she must have been five years old, at best. She smiled as she recalled her father picking her off the lawn and holding her in his arms. Even now, she missed him terribly.

She recalled the day at eleven years old when she returned home from school to be told that her father had died. Mildenheath's finest police officer and finest father, shot in a bungled bank robbery. The terror and desperation came back to her now as she experienced the emotions again, as though brand new.

As the first tear rolled down her cheek, Wendy, startled, opened her eyes. Thank goodness. The lights were still red and the traffic was still stationary. She looked to her left to see if the man with the piercing blue eyes was still there. As she turned her head to him, he reciprocated.

Alarmed, Wendy shot her head back to dead centre and concentrated hard on the red light ahead.

Why is he looking at me? What does he know? He knows, doesn't he? He can see the guilt. He knows what I've done to Michael. Oh shit, oh shit. Come on, fucking lights. Turn green, you bastards!

As though Wendy's power of concentration had worked, the lights turned green. But the traffic stayed still.

8

As WENDY GUIDED HER CAR ROUND THE HOSPITAL CAR park looking for a space, her head was filled with thoughts of what she might find inside.

Would Michael be conscious? Would he have tubes and lines sticking out of every orifice, just like last time? Surely not. He couldn't be as bad as he was last time. He wouldn't do that again. Three weeks in intensive care, his stomach pumped, his kidneys flushed, his face as grey as stone. Despite this, Michael showed no remorse and had made no attempt to turn his life around. This is what irritated Wendy the most. This was why she had seen her brother only a handful of times over the past few years. Wendy knew deep down that each time could well be the last.

As she traipsed up the unnecessarily long and winding disabled access ramp, last night's words rang in Wendy's ears.

I'm through with you, Michael. I don't want anything to do with you.

It was the only way I knew how to cope.

I'm through with you, Michael.

I'm trying! I swear to God I'm trying!

I'm through with you, Michael. I don't want anything to do with you.

I don't want anything to do with you.

The stench hit Wendy as soon as the automatic doors opened. It smelt of death and antiseptic. Wendy hated hospitals. The woman at the reception desk reminded her of a schoolteacher from a budget porn film, her dark-rimmed glasses perched on the edge of her nose, her suit blouse exposing far too much breast tissue for medically unstable patients to cope with. Tart. That might even be a health and safety issue.

The tart looked down her oh-so-perfect nose and informed Wendy that Michael was in bed number seven on the Egret ward. The tart's blunt manner led Wendy to believe that she knew exactly why Michael was in the ward. *Look at her, coming in here to visit her worthless drug addict brother.*

The nurse on the ward's reception desk updated Wendy on her brother's condition. He hadn't overdosed as originally thought, but had instead drunk two bottles of cheap brandy and fumbled around with a packet of painkillers before calling the police. A cry for help, they said. His stomach had been pumped and they were holding him under observation until they could let him go.

As Wendy entered the Egret ward, she scanned the walls for a laminated placard displaying the number seven. Two elderly gentlemen in beds one and two were comparing their abdominal scars whilst a Jamaican lady snored loudly from bed five. Two beds closer to Wendy, in bed number seven, lay Michael.

Michael was awake and looking at Wendy like a small child who knew he had done something terribly wrong. The helpless look on his face shook her to the core. She cantered over to bed seven and hugged Michael.

'Careful, sis. I've had all sorts of bloody lines and pumps hanging out of me. I'm a bit sore.'

'Oh, Michael. Why did you do this? Why?'

'Because I'm a fucking idiot, Wend. Because I couldn't cope with you leaving me again and I hated myself. I fucking hated myself.'

'How could you be so selfish, Michael?'

'Selfish? You want to talk to me about selfish? How many times have you come to visit me over the past few years, Wend? You're just as bad as dad was, devoting your entire life to the sodding police force and making everyone else take a back seat.'

Wendy bit her tongue. 'Michael, I have to work to live. My job is very important to me and it involves a lot of hard work. You've not exactly made much effort with me, either.'

'Is that the best you can do? You've seen me twice in eighteen months because your job involves a lot of work? Even dad used to be home to see us one or two nights a week.'

'Stop comparing me to dad, Michael!'

'Why the hell not? You're both the bloody same. All that matters is the police force and the rest of the world can go to hell.'

'Michael, you really need to understand that we're on the same side here. You're not to blame for being here in this hospital bed. The people to blame are the scum who push drugs onto vulnerable people and get them hooked, the people who use their filthy drug money to feed organised crime. The people who think nothing of being a rapist or a murderer. They are the people I have a responsibility to bring down, Michael. We're fighting the same battle.'

'I dunno, Wend. At the end of the day you're able to go home to your warm cosy little flat while I'm still out fighting on the streets. It's twenty-four seven for me, you know.'

'So join me. Come and stay with me in my "warm, cosy little flat" and I'll look after you. No more drugs, no more dealers knocking on the door, no more temptation.'

'What? Are you sure?'

Wendy almost regretted the offer as soon as she had made it. Was this really the right decision to be making? Getting involved in something like this could impact badly on her career. There it goes again – that word. Career. What does a career matter when your brother is dying slowly and painfully through a drug addiction? Wendy knew what she had to do.

'I'm sure, Michael. At the end of the day, you're still my brother.'

As she left the Egret ward with the Jamaican woman still blissfully snoring away, Wendy was on an emotional high. She knew she was the right person to look after Michael and to aid his recovery. What's more, she felt increasingly confident about being able to get to the bottom of the murders in Mildenheath. She hadn't felt this good in ages.

Fumbling through her pockets for her car keys, Wendy pulled out a crumpled business card.

Robert Ludford ~ Chartered Accountant.

She took her mobile phone from her jacket pocket and dialled the number.

'Hello, Robert?'

'Yes. Is that you, Wendy?'

'Yeah. Listen, I wanted to apologise for what I said on the phone earlier. I was out of order. I've been under a lot of stress recently and—'

ADAM CROFT

'It's fine, honestly. Apology accepted,' Robert said. She could almost hear him smiling.

'Thank you, Robert. Does the offer still stand?'

'Dinner? Of course it does.'

'Excellent. Shall we say tomorrow night?'

'I'll pick you up at eight.'

9

Tom Connors sat in silence as Culverhouse began to conduct the interview, having waited for Wendy to get back from the hospital before they continued.

'Tom, I'll cut straight to the chase. We'd like to speak with you about a young lady called Ella Barrington. We believe you may have known her,' Culverhouse said as he placed a photograph of Ella Barrington in front of Tom Connors.

'Suspect? You didn't say nothing about me being no suspect!' Tom said, panicked.

Wendy interjected. 'It's just police terminology, Tom. Just a thing we have to do, you know, or our bosses tell us off. Don't worry, you're not under arrest.'

Culverhouse shot a thankful smile at Wendy. 'Terminology, exactly. Tom, do you recognise this woman?'

Tom shuffled uncomfortably.

'No, I've never seen her before.'

'Are you sure?'

'Yes. I've never seen her before.'

Culverhouse sat in silence for a moment, wistfully planning his next move.

'Tom, do you recognise this woman? For the benefit of the tape, I am now showing the sus—Mr Connors a photograph of Maria Preston.'

He handed the photograph to Tom Connors. It looked as though it had been taken at a recent party. Fellow drunken revellers partied on behind her whilst she posed daintily for the camera, a single lock of blonde hair draped across her forehead, a symbol of the care-free attitude she must have had that night. It had been one of her last.

'No. I don't recognise her either.'

Culverhouse let out a slight involuntary grunt and glanced almost apologetically at Wendy. 'Tom, we've got *two* independent witnesses who've seen you with this woman on a number of occasions.'

Wendy was furious at Culverhouse's bending of the truth, but managed to remain calm. 'Guv... I don't think that's—'

'They're lying! You're lying! I've never seen her in my life! I swear!'

Culverhouse leaned over. 'Listen to me, Connors. I've got a routine for dealing with shits like you. I ask three polite questions and then it gets nasty. You've had two. What do you know about Ella Barrington and Maria Preston?'

Tom paused for a moment.

'They were prostitutes, weren't they? I mean, I saw it on the news. Look, I'd been seeing a girl for a little while. Her name was Gabriella Poulson. She was... one of them.'

'A prostitute?' Wendy asked.

Tom Connors looked uneasy at the mention of the word, but eventually nodded.

'Yeah. One of them. I went to her a few months back and started to get involved. Far too involved.'

'You mean you fell in love with her?'

'Sort of. I guess. I couldn't see enough of her. I started to see her every night and I'd buy her presents, jewellery and stuff.'

'Did that not get a bit expensive? I was under the impression you worked in a video rental shop,' Culverhouse asked.

'I do. I had some money saved up and I worked extra hours. It's strange, the things you do for... y'know...'

Wendy nodded sympathetically. From what she knew of Asperger's, she wondered what Tom Connors's interpretation of love would be, and almost felt added sympathy because of it.

'I understand.'

'Look, I wanna get something off my chest,' Tom continued. 'When I started to fall for Gabriella it began to dawn on me just what she was.'

'What do you mean, Tom?'

'The fact that she was... one of them. It seemed to matter more and more all the time. One night she came over to mine. She had clearly been to another bloke's house just before. Her lipstick was smudged and her underwear was skew-whiff. It felt like she had no respect for me and I just lost it.'

'You hit her?'

'Yeah,' Tom said after a few moments of silence. 'I hit her.'

Culverhouse leaned forward onto the interview desk, poised like an eagle stalking his prey.

'And what happened?'

'Well I didn't kill her if that's what you mean. She didn't say a word. Just packed up and left. It didn't strike me as being the first time it'd happened to her, if you get where I'm coming from. But listen, I've never seen any of those other two women before in my life. I swear.'

'OK Tom. We're going to need to check a few things with this Gabriella Poulson. Do you have any contact details for her?' Wendy asked.

'Not on me. She lives in digs on the Marshwood estate. Opposite the petrol station. Number 4a.'

'Right. I think we'd better go and corroborate your story. We'll keep you in a cell until we've backed the story up,' Culverhouse said.

'No! You can't keep me in here! Anyway, how can she back my story up if she's dead? What happens then?'

'Then you've got some explaining to do, Mr Connors.'

The Marshwood estate was notorious in Mildenheath. Gang culture had gripped the estate and cab drivers would no longer enter the estate for fear of being attacked by feral youths. The estate used to be served by two bus routes, the 34 and 62, but the local bus company had amended the routes to circumvent the estate entirely. To most, it seemed as though the Marshwood estate was cut off from the rest of Mildenheath entirely, like a cancerous growth just waiting to be lanced.

It was four o'clock in the afternoon when Wendy and Culverhouse pulled into the estate in their unmarked car. Entering the estate in a marked vehicle was completely out of the question. Two back-up officers sat on the edge of the estate in another unmarked car.

'A date?' Culverhouse said as they pulled up at the petrol station. It was the safest place to leave the car, Cuvlerhouse had declared. At least the petrol station would have CCTV.

'Yeah, with a guy I bumped into in the pub the other night. He's an accountant.'

'An accountant? Right.'

'Is there a problem?'

'No, no problem. Just make sure you keep your attention focused solely on the case, Knight. I don't want any lovey-dovey bullshit out of you until we've found our man. There's only one person I want getting nailed at the moment, and it ain't you.'

They made their way towards the block of flats opposite the petrol station. It was fortunate that Tom Connors had referred to it in this way as the building lacked any other sort of identification. No name plaque, no road signs, nothing. Just another grey, soulless building opposite a petrol station. Stepping over discarded chip paper and lager cans, Wendy and Culverhouse entered the building.

The entrance hall was cold and dark, a staircase scaling the right-hand wall before turning to climb the wall opposite the door. A teenage couple, no older than fourteen, sat on the concrete apex with faces interlocked and their hands where God only knew.

Hidden behind the staircase, with the concrete apex and canoodling couple only inches above them, was number 4a. Wendy inadvertently scanned the door for the most germ-free spot before knocking firmly.

The door was eventually answered by a woman with a drawn complexion, her drug-abused skin hanging desperately from her bony cheeks.

'Gabriella Poulson?'

'Who's asking?'

'DCI Culverhouse and DS Wendy Knight, Mildenheath Police.'

Gabriella moved to slam the door but Culverhouse's size eleven boots were already firmly placed against the doorframe.

'We're not here to arrest you, love. You know what you are and I know what you are, but we need you to help us with our investigation.'

'Why the hell should I help you lot?'

'Because two prostitutes have been murdered in Mildenheath and we reckon he's about to do a third. If you don't want to end up being the next, you'd better start talking to us.'

Gabriella paused before opening the door and motioning for Wendy and Culverhouse to enter the flat before anyone spotted them.

The line between the flat and the street was non-existent. Lager cans and food packets were strewn across the flat along with a selection of used syringes and condoms.

'Christ, you running an AIDS factory in here or something?' Culverhouse said.

They walked over to the lounge corner and Culverhouse daintily scoured the rotting sofa for somewhere safe to sit. Once he had done so, he dusted his knees and looked up to see Wendy quite content with standing.

'Gabriella, we need you to tell us if you know a gentleman by the name of Tom Connors,' Wendy said.

'Tom?' she said, thinking. 'Yeah, he was a client of mine.'

'Was?'

'Yeah, was. Until it got too much for him and he decided to lump me one,' she said, snorting through her nose.

'Did you not go to the police about it?' Wendy asked.

'What's the point? They never do nothing. Not exactly sympathetic about people like us.'

'Is it something you want us to follow up?'

'I'm not pressing charges if that's what you mean,' Gabriella said, folding her arms in a show of defiance.

'Was Tom ever... more than a client to you, Gabriella?' Wendy asked.

'Nah. I was probably more than just another hooker to him, but it was purely business from my point of view.'

'And do you know either of these girls?' Culverhouse asked, handing Gabriella the photographs of Ella Barrington and Maria Preston.

'Na. Never seen either of them before.'

'Are you sure? It's very important,' Wendy asked.

'Are these them two girls what got killed?'

'Yes,' Culverhouse said.

'Ah, I see. So because they was hookers too, you must've thought we all knew each other. Sorry, Inspector. Doesn't quite work like that. A bloody shame, but I've never seen them. Honest.'

'Right. Well thanks for your time.'

Culverhouse, clearly intent on not spending a second longer than he had to in Gabriella's flat, marched off towards the door. Wendy watched him leave before offering some words of advice to Gabriella.

'Just… be careful, OK? He's out there and he's going to kill again. Please make sure you're not the next one.'

As she left the flat, Wendy found Culverhouse stood near the entrance to the building, motioning towards the concrete apex.

'Disgusting, ain't it? Not even out of nappies and they're already fumbling around like a Jew in a Christmas shop.'

On leaving the building, Culverhouse checked the car still had four wheels and six windows before his phone rang.

'Culverhouse,' he barked, answering it.

'Guv, it's Frank. We've got another body.'

'Christ almighty. Does it match the MO?'

'It seems to. Funny thing is the body's still warm. Early word is it's happened in the last couple of hours. So it can't possibly have been Tom Connors.'

'Brilliant. Just fucking brilliant.' Culverhouse snapped the phone shut and shoved it into his jacket pocket.

'What's up?'

'That was DS Vine. They've found another body. It wasn't Connors. It's still warm.'

'Shit. There goes another evening to myself,' Wendy said, thinking of what she'd say to Robert.

'Nonsense,' Culverhouse said, taking her by the arm. 'You've been working flat out since yesterday morning. You need a break. Go on your date.'

Wendy smiled.

10

THE PERFUME SMELLED SWEETER THAN USUAL AS WENDY delicately sprayed the sides of her neck. But then again it had been a while since she'd worn perfume, hadn't it? At least six months? It must have been.

She turned to look at the four dresses which hung from the door of her wardrobe. A simple choice, but impossible to make. To the left, a long, white dress decorated with a rose pattern and a black horizontal band. Too flowery. Next to it, a short black number with a sequinned bust line. Too slutty. She eyed the grey linen one with the collar and chest pockets. Too frumpy. That left the tight green one with the plunging v-neck bust. Process of elimination. Good police work.

Selecting appropriate jewellery wasn't much easier, either. It occurred to Wendy that it had been far too long since she'd been on a date. Almost two years, in fact. Since she had been concentrating so hard on her career, she'd had no time for boyfriends.

All that matters is the police force and the rest of the world can go to hell.

Just as Wendy had selected the diamond-encrusted watch and matching earrings, the taxi honked its horn, perfectly on cue.

'Well, here goes nothing,' she said to herself as she descended the staircase.

Wendy arrived at Alessandro's to find Robert Ludford already seated at a table for two. The table was topped with a single red rose and a bottle of *Veuve Clicquot* was nestled in a bucket of ice.

Alessandro's had been one of her favourite restaurants for years. It'd been in the town for over thirty of them already, and could certainly be considered for the "hidden gem" status which so many tourists sought. Not that Mildenheath was exactly a tourist destination.

'Good evening, Wendy. You look beautiful.'

'Thank you, Robert,' she said gracefully as if getting ready had been no effort at all.

'I took the liberty of ordering us some champagne. I hope you don't mind.'

'No, of course not. That's lovely, thank you.'

Wendy felt distinctly out of place as she perused the menu at Alessandro's. She suddenly realised how long it had been since she'd been here, and what her life had become since. Chicken liver pate served with toasted bread and berry compote. King prawns sautéed in olive oil, garlic and chillies, served with fresh bread. King scallops and king prawns in a white wine and cream sauce infused with chilli. *No microwave ready meals for one here, girl.*

'What will you have, Robert?'

"I'm thinking perhaps *Il Risotto al Funghi Porcini*."

'My favourite,' Wendy said, innocently. 'I'll have the same.'

'Marvellous. So, tell me about this investigation.'

'Sorry?'

'The serial killer case. I presume it's the one you're on. I've read about it in the papers. Terrible thing to happen.'

'Yes, it is. I can't really speak about it though, I'm sure you understand.'

'Of course,' Robert said, smiling. 'Do you have any suspects?'

Wendy smiled and exhaled in resignation.

'Why are you so keen to know?'

'No reason. It doesn't matter.'

'Of course it does,' Wendy replied, taking a sip of champagne.

'But it sounds so silly.'

Wendy took his hand, sensing that he wanted to say something. 'Tell me, Robert.'

'Right, well, if you promise not to laugh.'

'Promise.'

'I like to write in my spare time. Novels, you know. I really enjoy writing crime novels about serial killers and murders. It's stupid, I know. But now you know.'

A slight titter escaped Wendy's mouth, not unnoticed by her date.

'Wendy, you promised you wouldn't laugh,' he said, his pride clearly dented.

'Oh Robert, I'm not laughing at that. I'm laughing at how you dressed it up as some big secret.'

'You mean you don't find it weird or sad?'

'Of course not. In fact, I find it kind of sexy.'

'Sexy?' Robert asked, smiling.

'Well, someone who writes crime novels must have quite a creative imagination…' Wendy glanced at the label on the back of the bottle of champagne. 'Sorry, I didn't mean to sound so forward. I'm not usually like this, I promise.'

'Well, I like to think it was my masculine charm rather than the alcohol,' Robert said, noting where her eyes had darted to.

'Of course. I'm sorry. I know I've only had one glass but I drink much faster when I'm nervous.'

'What is there to be nervous about?'

'Not nervous. Excited.'

Robert smiled.

A few minutes later, the waiter floated to the table carrying two plates of *Il Risotto al Funghi Porcini* which he placed in front of the two diners.

I hate mushrooms! And where's the bloody meat?!

'Everything OK, Wendy?'

'Yes! Looks delicious!'

Wendy tucked into her festering fungus and cheesy gloop, eager not to upset her companion for the evening.

'So, Robert. Are you not married?' It seemed a daft question to ask on a date, but Wendy had been caught out before.

'Me? No. Well, I was. Separated, I guess you might say.'

'Oh, I'm sorry to hear that,' she replied, wanting to know more but not wanting to ask more.

'Isn't everyone? Truth is it just wasn't working out between us. We tried to keep it together but in the end we'd drifted so far apart she ended up going off with someone else.'

Wendy sat in silence, safe in the knowledge that silence made people talk.

'I suppose I'm just like any other guy, you know? No man is an island. I guess I just want to be happy and feel loved again.'

Wendy smiled and said no more.

At the end of the evening, Wendy and Robert left the restaurant and hailed a taxi. As the taxi pulled up outside Wendy's house, she felt an insatiable urge, leaning over and kissing Robert passionately before getting out of the taxi and heading into her house before saying another word.

Once inside, Wendy nursed a glass of red wine. A million thoughts flew through her head, but above all she realised she must stick to her promise to be completely open with Michael about everything. After all they'd been through, their sibling relationship had to be built on a foundation of trust. She'd decided. She'd tell him about her blossoming relationship with Robert.

11

THE INCIDENT ROOM WAS EERILY QUIET AT FIVE-THIRTY the next morning. DCI Jack Culverhouse sat slumped over a manila file and a mug of strong black coffee. He had trouble sleeping at the best of times but he knew he would not be able to rest until he had caught the killer of the three women.

Ever since he had been on his own, Jack Culverhouse had become increasingly obsessed with work. His wife had told him that had been the case for years, but Jack knew that was nothing compared to now. The truth was that working dulled the pain. The pain of having your wife of almost twenty years leave you in the dead of night with your only child. That sort of thing could finish a man. But not Jack.

He thought about Emily every day. She would be almost twelve years old by now. He had done everything in his power to track down Helen and her successive string of male partners in order to get access to his daughter but every new lead came to a dead end. He didn't give two shits about his wife; he just wanted to see Emily. Desperately.

He took another slurp of coffee as he contemplated his next move on the case. The manila file beneath his left elbow seemed to be growing almost by the minute. Growing with information on more redundant leads and phone calls from deadheads who were convinced they could solve the murders using a range of mysterious techniques. Dowsers, tarot card readers, psychics; they were all there, all willing to help. All willing to waste Jack's fucking time.

The phone rang. Jack glanced at the clock. Eight-fifteen. He wondered for a moment why he couldn't sleep at home in his super-king-size bed but had no trouble dozing off when he was leaning on a pile of papers and a coffee mug.

'Culverhouse,' he said, cradling the receiver.

'Jack, it's Charles Hawes.'

Jack, eh? That's a good start. *Looks like we're on friendly terms today*, he thought.

'Ah. Good morning, Chief Constable.'

'Can you come and see me in my office please, Jack?'

'I've got a team briefing in fifteen minutes, sir. Shall I pop up after?'

'Now, Culverhouse.'

Culverhouse, now, is it? Bang goes the friendship, then.

As DCI Culverhouse made his way up the concrete staircase to the Chief Constable's office, he feared the worst. Pausing to knock gingerly on the door, Culverhouse entered the office. The Chief Constable was stood with his back to him, arms folded, looking out of his large window onto the streets of Mildenheath.

'Sit down, Jack. What's the latest on the serial murder case?'

'No news, sir. We had a suspect in for questioning, but it looks like we're going to have to let him go.'

'So I hear,' Hawes said, turning and perching on the edge of his desk. 'I also hear that we've had another murder take place while the suspect was with us.'

'That's correct, sir.'

'So tell me. What made you interview Tom Connors in the first place, Culverhouse?'

Jack swallowed hard as he felt the tension rising. The Chief Constable was using his surname again.

'We had a tip-off from someone who said he knew Maria Preston and had reason to believe he may have somehow been involved in her death, sir.'

Hawes nodded. 'His mum, I hear.'

'That's correct, sir.'

'You do realise it's now been two full days without as much as the slightest breakthrough? I mean, I wasn't expecting you to have the case wrapped up and someone in court within forty-eight hours, but this is starting to take the piss. We have three girls dead and you think it's a good idea to go round and have tea with every little old lady who thinks their son's been a naughty boy. Just what the hell are you playing at, Jack?'

'Sir, at the time we had reason to believe Tom Connors may have been involved in Maria Preston's death.'

'Oh, really? Well let's just hope the IPCC agree with you.'

'IPCC, sir?'

'Yes, Jack. Tom Connors has made a formal complaint over yesterday's little episode. Let me tell you now, if we don't get results — and fast — you're going to be out of this building quicker than you can say "Two sugars, please, Mrs Connors". Do I make myself clear?'

'Crystal, sir.'

Culverhouse left the office with the Chief Constable's words ringing in his ears as he made his way back down to the incident room, late for the team briefing.

'Here he is!' called the familiar voice of DS Steve Wing. 'Overslept did we, guv?'

The incident room was momentarily awash with titters before the eyes settled on Culverhouse. His body language said everything.

'In fact, DS Wing, I've just been to see the Chief Constable.'

'Bad news, guv?'

"Quite the opposite. It could be fucking fantastic news for Chief Constable Hawes if he gets to roast my bollocks on his barbecue at the weekend. We need results and fast.

I've just had the dressing down of my life from the Hawes and if we don't start making some serious inroads in this investigation, we're all for it. The fact of the matter is we're now averaging a killing a day. Every day we let this bastard stay on the streets, another girl dies. Frank, did you get an ID on the third victim in the end?'

DS Frank Vine grabbed a file from his desk and took out his notes.

'Yes, guv. Nicole Bryant, aged seventeen. It seems as though she was a college student.'

'Same MO as the previous two?'

'Identical, sir.'

'So we're looking at another prostitute, then?'

'There's no evidence to say so, guv.'

' don't need evidence to say so, Frank. Have the next-of-kin been informed?'

'There's an FLO with the family as we speak, guv.'

'Right, well I'm going to go round and have a word with Mr and Mrs Bryant myself. Speed things up a bit.'

'Are you sure that's wise, guv?'

'Why would it not be? Did you not hear a word I said about Hawes?'

'Well, I mean, if you're going to be following this bee you've got in your bonnet about her being a prostitute…'

'Detective Sergeant Vine, I am perfectly capable of exercising tact. Now, whether you like it or not, I'm going to visit Little Miss Secret-Hooker's parents. If it helps you sleep at night, I'll take DS Knight with me. Knight, get your coat.'

A wolf-whistle emanated from the direction of DS Steve Wing. Fortunately, it went either unheard or ignored by Culverhouse.

12

Wendy could hear the breath rushing through Culverhouse's nostrils as they approached the Bryant household on Mayfield Avenue that afternoon. She decided an element of tact was required.

'Guv, please tell me you're not planning to bring up this whole prostitute thing with her parents.'

'I think they have a bloody good right to know, Knight. Wouldn't you want to know if your daughter was a hooker?'

'But don't know that at the moment. Just because the other girls were prostitutes doesn't mean that Nicole was one too. It's perfectly common for a serial killer to deviate from his MO as he gets more and more confident with his killings.'

'I've made my own mind up about what's *perfectly common*, thank you very much, Knight.'

Wendy sighed and shook her head as Culverhouse plunged his finger into the recesses of the Bryants' doorbell. Moments later, a sombre looking man with wispy grey hair, although one could tell from his face he was no older than sixty, opened the door. Immediately, Culverhouse's attitude changed.

'Mr Bryant?'

'Yes.'

'Detective Chief Inspector Culverhouse and Detective Sergeant Knight. We're here about your daughter. We're terribly sorry for the shock you must have had.'

The man seemed somewhat subdued and numb. 'Oh. Oh, right. Yes, come on in.'

As they made their way into the living room, Wendy observed that it probably hadn't been decorated since the mid-1970s. If it had, perhaps browns, purples and swathes of filigree were back in fashion again and it was *her* that was out of touch.

'Mrs Bryant, hello. I'm DCI Jack Culverhouse and this is DS Wendy Knight.'

'Please, call me Patricia.'

Different people deal with grief in different ways, but Wendy noticed that Patricia and Gerry Bryant seemed somewhat emotionless that afternoon. It's not that they weren't sad; they weren't *anything*. They seemed numb, almost like plastic figurines or the subjects of a government drug experiment.

'Mrs Bryant, I realise it must be difficult for you but we need to ask some rather... direct... questions about Nicole.'

Before Mrs Bryant could comprehend Culverhouse's remark, Wendy placed a controlling hand on his arm and took over the lead of questioning.

'I think what my DCI is trying to say, Mrs Bryant, is that there are some links between Nicole's death and those of some other girls in the area recently and we have to investigate a possible connection as a matter of course.'

'Links? You mean... a serial killer?'

'It's far too early to say at this stage, but we do need to investigate the links.'

'What sort of links?' Gerry Bryant interjected.

'Well, what sort of insight did you have into your daughter's social life?'

'We didn't see her all that often, if I'm honest. Patricia and I have never been to her current home as I don't drive and Patricia finds it difficult to walk long distances with her knees.' Wendy mentally adjusted her calculation of the Bryants' ages. 'Nicole is... was... always too busy with work to be able to pop over much so we more or less conducted most of our relationship over the telephone.'

'Why did Nicole live away from home? I mean, seventeen is quite a young age to set up on your own without any sort of boyfriend, isn't it?'

'She was an independent woman.'

Culverhouse's eyebrow rose at this last word.

'Yes, Inspector. A woman. That is how I saw my daughter. She was very mature and we had no qualms about helping her set up on her own.'

'What sort of work did she do, Mr Bryant?' Wendy asked.

'I don't know. She didn't say much to either of us about it. I think she was a little embarrassed.'

Wendy's eyes met Culverhouse's. As Culverhouse opened his mouth to speak, Wendy decided it was best if she continued.

'Embarrassed about what, Mr Bryant?'

'Please, call me Gerry. I don't know what she was embarrassed about. I got the impression she'd had to take up work in a shop of some sort after she lost her office job. She was a very proud woman, Detective Sergeant. It would have pained her to take any sort of menial employment, never mind having to tell her parents about it.'

'Do you know for certain that it was a shop job?'

'Not for certain, no.'

'Did it involve unsociable hours, do you know?'

'It's hard to say. We used to speak to her at different times of day on the telephone but I assumed it was because she was part-time or on that flexi-hours thing.'

'Is it possible that Nicole might have been mixed up in some sort of additional work or something she might not have wanted to tell anyone?' Culverhouse asked.

'As I said, she wouldn't have wanted to tell anyone if she had a menial job. She was very proud.'

'I'm not talking about pride, Mr Bryant. I'm talking about whether her job was socially or legally acceptable.'

Gerry Bryant looked confused; Jack Culverhouse looked exasperated.

'I'm sorry, I'm not quite sure what you mean.'

'Oh, for crying out loud, man! Were you born with your head up your arse? Was your daughter a prossie or what?'

'Jack!' Wendy barked.

'I beg your pardon, Detective Chief Inspector! Just what are you insinuating?'

Patricia Bryant showed the first signs of emotion as she began to howl with tears.

'I am insinuating, Mr Bryant, that your daughter was killed in a very similar manner to, and very probably by the same person as, a couple of prostitutes we've found dead round here recently. Now, I couldn't give a rat's arse if your precious daughter was on the game or not, but if it turns out to be the missing link that stops us from catching whoever killed these three women, I'm not going to be a very happy bunny.'

Gerry Bryant rose slowly to his feet, his hands shaking and his face turning a deep shade of red.

'Get *out*! Get out of my house! I won't have that sort of talk around here!'

Wendy tried to pacify the situation.

'Mr Bryant, I'm sure DCI Culverhouse is very sorry. If we could just—'

'Just *nothing*! *Get out of my house!*'

Although Gerry Bryant was technically obliged to provide any evidence which may be useful to the case, Wendy felt the safest option would be to head back and see the Bryants once they'd had a chance to cool down, and she'd had a chance to make sure Culverhouse wasn't within twenty miles.

'Nice one, Knight,' Culverhouse said as the door slammed behind them.

'I beg your pardon? What did I do wrong?'

'We need to get evidence from that man to help our investigation. If we don't find out whether or not Nicole Bryant was a hooker, we could end up scraping another dead body off the streets tomorrow morning and I'll be for the fucking chopping block when Chief Constable Hawes finds out.'

'Perhaps if you'd managed to exercise a bit of tact, we might have got the evidence we wanted. Unfortunately I don't have a time machine which can stop anyone else getting murdered in the meantime, nor can I go back to five minutes ago and put some sodding gaffer tape round your mouth, so I'd appreciate it — no, I *demand*, that you let me deal with witnesses and grieving families from now on, Inspector.'

Culverhouse stopped dead in his tracks.

'You *demand*, DS Knight?'

'Yes, sir,' Wendy said, a little more subdued. 'I demand.'

'You kinky bitch.'

After dropping Culverhouse back at the station that afternoon, Wendy drove to the hospital.

Her mind was overflowing with mixed feelings as she walked towards Michael's ward. Was it wise to bring a recovering addict back into her home? What's to say he was even recovering? Was it really worth jeopardising her career? The angel on her opposite shoulder kicked the devil into touch, declaring that Michael was family and families stuck together. *Except when they go and die on you.*

Walking onto the ward, Wendy noticed that Michael looked much better than he had the last time she saw him. He looked fit, happy and healthy.

'Ah, my chauffeur! Betty, this is my sister, Wendy.'

Wendy shook the nurse's hand.

'You look much better, Michael.'

'I feel better, Wend. It's amazing how being forced into a situation makes you to come to terms with the way you saw things before. Sometimes it's only when someone forces you into that situation that you actually see the world for what it really is.'

'Painkillers talking?'

Michael smiled. 'Something like that.'

'Come on, then. Let's get you out of here. I've got a lamb joint in for tonight.'

'Lamb! You remembered!'

'How could I forget? You used to run around the house like a delirious lunatic every time mum cooked lamb.'

'That was probably a reaction to the foul smell it makes when it's cooking. You don't mind if I keep well away from the kitchen before dinner, do you?'

'As long as you eat it all, I don't care, because you're not getting any pudding unless you do.'

Michael gestured a sarcastic salute. 'Yes, ma'am!'

13

As WENDY'S CAR PASSED THROUGH MILDENHEATH AND
the formality of the hospital setting faded into the rear-
view mirror, a sullen air of silence fell over her and Michael
as reality began to set in.

'So, how's work?' Michael asked, eventually.

'Yeah, fine. Working on a big case at the moment so I'm
glad to have you at home where I can keep an eye on you.'

'Yeah? How so?'

'Well, it's a lot easier than trekking to the hospital all
the time, especially as I can't guarantee I'll be free during
visiting times.'

'No, I meant the big case. What's it all about?'

'Ah, you know,' she said with an air of false joking. 'Madman on the loose bludgeoning young girls to death. The usual fare.'

'Just another day in the town of Mildenheath, then?'

'Something like that,' Wendy replied, smiling.

'And how's the love life?'

'You think I get time for one of those with work?'

'Probably not, seeing as you tend to be so obsessed with it.'

'I am *not* obsessed with work, Michael. Being a police officer isn't just a job, you know. It's a way of life. You can't just switch off at five o'clock and lock the office door.'

'Yeah, but does it need to get in the way of your social life?'

'It doesn't. I don't have a social life, Michael,' she said, half-smiling.

'Well yeah, exactly. You used to, though. You were always bringing boys back to the house when we were at upper school. Now, you've barely got time for your own brother, let alone anyone else.'

'That's just not true, Michael,' Wendy replied, hurt. She brooded in silence for a few moments before speaking again. 'As a matter of fact, I've met someone.'

'Oh?'

'His name's Robert.'

'Good start.'

'Yes, well. That's exactly what it is: a good start. It's still early days and I don't know if anything will come of it but

I thought you ought to know. If we're going to get this all sorted out, we both need to be totally open and honest with each other.'

'I'm delighted for you, Wend. Why don't you invite him over?'

'What, are you sure? Are you ready for that?'

'I'll be honest, sis; I've had bigger emotional shocks in my life than my sister telling me she's got a new boyfriend.'

'I didn't mean emotionally, you berk. I meant physically.'

'Well I didn't think I was going to have to challenge him to a duel, if that's what you mean,' Michael said, joking. Wendy simply smiled. Michael's sense of humour was returning. Good sign. 'I'm fine, Wend. Physically, too.'

'Well, if you're sure, that would be lovely. And I promise I won't buy lamb.'

'Oh, but I like lamb,' Michael said. 'It's just the smell it makes when it cooks that I can't stand.'

'Exactly. You're cooking.'

For the first time in as long as she could remember, Wendy truly felt as though everything in her life was improving. Well, almost everything. Although it was still very early to say, Michael seemed to be getting better and she had met a truly alluring man in Robert Ludford. She remained haunted, though, by the prospect of there being another girl murdered before the killer could be caught. A positive outlook would help her, she decided. If her private life was going well, her work life would follow, surely?

14

IT WAS JUST AFTER NINE O'CLOCK IN THE MORNING WHEN the phone rang in the incident room at Mildenheath CID. Culverhouse answered it with his usual grunt.

'DCI Culverhouse?' the voice on the other end of the line asked. 'It's Gerry Bryant, here.'

'Ah. Mr Bryant. Listen, I...'

'Look, I just wanted to call and apologise for yesterday.'

'*You* wanted to apologise?'

'Yes. I was completely out of order. I should never have spoken to you like that and thrown you out of the house.'

'No, well. Let's... make sure it never happens again, yes?' Culverhouse replied, confused.

'Very well, Inspector. To bring us back to your original question, though...'

Culverhouse racked his brain, but he couldn't remember having asked Gerry Bryant any questions during their brief telephone conversation.

'My question?'

'Yes. You wanted to know if Nicole was a... was one of those. You know.'

'Oh,' Culverhouse said, suddenly remembering. 'A prostitute, Mr Bryant?'

'Yes. Well, no. That's just it. I can absolutely categorically say she wasn't.'

'Well, I respect your views, Mr Bryant, but how can you *categorically* say that? You admitted yourself that you very rarely saw or spoke to Nicole.'

'Yes, but that doesn't change the facts. Nicole had — has — a sister. None of us see her any more. I think she's in London, now. At least that's where she said she was going. Bethany *was* a prostitute. Nicole despised that and hated it even more for tearing her family apart. The truth is, Inspector, you're not the first person to have the honour of being thrown out of my house.'

'You threw Bethany out?' Culverhouse asked.

'I didn't have a choice. She got mixed up in the drugs game too and it's not the sort of world I want infesting my household. Nicole agreed wholeheartedly and was often even more vehemently opposed to prostitution than I am. That, Inspector, is how I *know* Nicole wasn't mixed up in that terrible business and it's also why I reacted in the way I did. My wife and I have lost one daughter through prostitution and now, when our second one is murdered, you accuse her of being a prostitute as well. That cuts very deeply, especially as nothing could be further from the truth.'

Culverhouse let out an audible sigh. 'I understand, Mr Bryant. I'm sure you realise that we cannot entirely remove the possibility from our enquiries, but I can assure you that we will certainly focus our efforts elsewhere for the time being.'

'Thank you, Inspector. I would appreciate that.'

DS Wing was stood behind Culverhouse as he put the phone down.

'Gerry Bryant, guv?'

'Yes. He rang to *apologise*.'

'Apologise? With all due respect, guv, from what I've heard it's you who was meant to be apologising.'

'Yes, exactly. I'm not sure what's going on with Mr Bryant, Steve, but something's not quite right. I mean, it's a convenient little story, but why wouldn't he have said something about it to me at the time? Do me a favour, Steve. Have a look on HOLMES for anything about a Bethany Bryant. If she really existed and was into drugs and prostitution, I should imagine she'll have some sort of record.'

15

For the first time in a long time, Wendy felt young again. It was something she used to do a lot: getting ready for a big night with music playing as she got dressed and applied her make-up. Back in the day, it had been the three of them: Wendy, Emma and Michelle. The three musketeers, as they called themselves. Friends since lower school, and that was the way it would always be. Of course, it never happened that way. University, work and husbands had all got in the way. Emma and Michelle still saw each other fairly regularly, mainly because their husbands worked together. Wendy, though, had never been married and wasn't really involved with the girls any more. There had been no falling out; they had just drifted apart. Perhaps her work really had got in the way, she thought.

Michael poked his head round the corner of the bedroom door.

'Are you going to put a dress on under that belt or are you going to wear it as it is?'

'That 'belt' *is* my dress, thank you very much, Michael.'

'I know. I'm only joking. I just didn't realise they made dresses that short any more.'

Wendy felt a little unnerved by Michael's comment. She carefully caressed her hair with her hair brush. 'What, do you think it's *too* short? I mean, it is only a second date, after all.'

'Well, some might say it's *conveniently* short,' Michael replied with a wry smile.

'Oi!'

Michael managed to duck just in time as the hairbrush crashed into the wall behind him.

'Woah, woah! I'm sure the bel— dress will be fine, Wend. It's kind of cool, actually.'

'I wouldn't go that far. It's just some bargain-basement thing I picked up in the charity shop.'

'Nah, not the dress. I mean this. Us getting on like we used to. Bit of banter, and all that. Reminds me of when we were younger.'

'Well, there's more where that came from if you fancy making another remark about my dress sense.'

'I think I'll pass. So, are you keen on this Robert bloke then? Think he might be *the one*?' he said, in a swooning, thespian manner.

'Who knows? I'm not particularly fussed either way. If it works, it works. If not, hey.'

'What time's he coming?'

'Drugs addled your brain? I must have told you twenty times already. He should be here about seven-thirty.'

'Really? It's already seven-thirty-five.'

'Oh my God! It can't be!' Wendy scrambled across the bed and yanked the alarm clock towards her. *19:03*. As she read the digits for a second time, she heard Michael laugh out loud behind her. Had the clock not been plugged in at the wall it would have nestled nicely beside the hairbrush.

The doorbell rang on the stroke of seven-thirty and Wendy moved out into the hallway, halting at the full-length mirror to examine herself one last time. She turned to the door, then back to the mirror. She yanked the dress down two inches. Michael's words popped into her head: *conveniently short*. With that, Wendy pulled the dress up four inches and opened the door.

'Wendy! Wow!" Robert Ludford had a huge grin on his face, his head bobbing like a slow-motion pigeon as he eyed-up Wendy, a thousand naughty thoughts racing through his mind. Wendy stepped forward and pulled him into a hug. Robert hoped she hadn't noticed his rather unfortunate trouser bulge.

'I'm so glad you've come.'

Robert yelped and pulled out of the hug. 'Huh? What?'

'To the meal, Robert. I'm glad you've come,' Wendy replied, confused.

'Oh. Right. Yes. Me too.'

Slightly unnerved, Wendy stepped aside and let Robert in.

'I'd like you to meet someone, actually. Do you remember I was telling you about my brother, Michael?'

'I do indeed.'

'Michael, meet Robert, my date for the evening.'

Michael and Robert shook hands and greeted each other.

'Less of this "date" nonsense, Wend. I don't want to feel like the spare part!'

'Don't worry about that. We'll try and keep our hands out of each others' pants until we've finished dinner.'

Robert laughed nervously. 'So, umm... Michael. How are you?'

'Am I off the drugs, you mean?'

'Well, no, I meant "how are you". I don't...'

'It's OK, Robert,' Wendy said. 'I've told Michael that you know about the problems.'

'Ah. OK. Well yes, how is that going? Wendy said you were clean now.'

'Yeah, fine, thanks. I'm on a treatment program and my surrogate mother here is doing a grand job of keeping an overbearing eye on me. Except when she's at work, of course.'

'Yes, Michael gets up to all sorts of mischief when I'm at work. Yesterday he even did the ironing *and* the washing,' Wendy said.

'Well, that's more than I do so I'd be happy with that if I were you!' Robert said, laughing.

Wendy tried not to look more than a little bit disappointed. She wondered whether all women inherently and subconsciously considered marriage with every potential partner they met or if it was just an over-keen trait of hers.

Later that evening, the trio sat down to dinner and the red wine flowed, a Simply Red album playing on repeat in the next room.

'Just the one glass for me, please, Wendy. I have to drive back home tonight,' Robert said as Wendy started to pour the wine into his glass.

'Work in the morning?' Michael asked.

'No, I'm not in until Monday now.'

'Well, why don't you stay over then?'

Robert looked at Wendy.

'We've got room, haven't we, Wend?' Michael added.

'Well, yes…' Wendy replied.

'I wouldn't want to impose,' Robert said, sensing an air of awkwardness.

'No, that's fine, Robert. Michael's right. I can sleep on the sofa and you can have my bed.'

'Oh, nonsense. The sofa's fine for me.'

'I won't hear of it. Anyway, I prefer the sofa. It's probably comfier than the bed, actually.'

'Well, if you're sure. That would be very kind, thank you.'

'Good, because we're nearly at the end of the bottle.' Wendy poured another generous measure of wine into Robert's glass and smiled at him.

Later, as Wendy opened the third bottle of wine, the conversation began to flow just as well.

'So, how's the big case going?' Robert asked.

'Ah, not too well if I'm honest. There've been three murders now. We thought we had a link but it doesn't look like the third one matches. All this stuff's in the papers. I can't really tell you anything which hasn't been officially released.'

'How do you know it's the same guy?'

'We have our ways of knowing. We don't even know that it is a guy.'

Robert stuttered. 'W…well, no. But one assumes, doesn't one?'

'Indeed,' Wendy replied. 'Police work is 99% assumption.'

'And the other 1%?'

'Guesswork.'

'Enough to fill the public with confidence!' Michael added.

'So what doesn't match?' Robert asked.

'I really shouldn't be telling you both this. It's confidential stuff.'

'Oh, come on. You can tell us! We might even be able to help. Three heads are better than one, and all that.'

'OK, well, most if it's already been in the papers. But the first two victims were prostitutes. Known to the police, too, so that's indisputable.'

'Right...' Robert said.

'But the third one wasn't.'

'Really?'

'Yes. The funny thing is, though, her *sister* is a prostitute.'

Robert accidentally dropped his fork onto his plate.

'Her *sister*?'

'Yes. But she's alive and well in London and hasn't been to Mildenheath in years. We've checked with the Met.'

'I see,' Robert said. 'Interesting. If you'll excuse me for a moment, I just need to nip to the loo.'

Michael began to chew his beef more slowly as he watched Robert walk off towards the bathroom.

'How... odd,' Wendy remarked.

'Indeed,' Michael said. 'Very odd.'

Once the fourth bottle of wine had been drained, and as Wendy and Robert sat on the sofa, Michael declared that it was about time he went to bed. As the latch on Michael's bedroom door snapped shut, Robert put his arm round Wendy as she rested her head on his shoulder.

'I've had a lovely evening. Thank you.'

'It's been a pleasure. I'm just glad you could come.'

Robert chuckled to himself.

'What?'

'No, no. That just reminded me. You said that when I turned up earlier tonight and I thought you meant something else.'

'What do you mean?'

'Well, you opened the door stood in that sexy little black dress and I must admit I got a bit... aroused. The next thing I know, you've flung your arms around me and told me you were glad I'd come.'

Wendy spluttered with laughter as she tried to stop herself propelling red wine across the sofa.

'Robert! You have a dirty mind!'

'Well, you can't blame me. You look absolutely breathtaking in that dress.'

'Makes you *aroused*, you say? How do you mean?' Wendy asked, moving her hand up the inside of his leg. As she got to the top, she cupped his crotch in her hand and squeezed gently. 'Oh... that's how you mean...'

Wendy kissed Robert's neck as he groaned with pleasure. Standing to pull the bolt across on the living room door, Wendy lifted her dress an extra inch or two, revealing a distinct lack of underwear. With that, she straddled Robert on the sofa and they made love.

16

THE INCIDENT ROOM BUZZED WITH THE SHRILL RINGING of umpteen telephones permeating the very matter inside Wendy's brain. She found she couldn't even handle simple maths. She was sure there were six glasses of wine in the average bottle. *Four times six is twenty-four. Or is it? Let's just say it is. Twenty-four divided by three is eight. Fuck. Eight glasses of wine each. No wonder I've got a hangover. Wait, maybe I've done the maths wrong.*

'Seventeen hundred quid's worth of bloody jewellery!' Culverhouse screamed.

Umpteen shrieking phones or one shrieking Culverhouse? It was a tough choice.

'Sorry, guv?'

'That's SOCO's take on what that Bryant bird was wearing when she kicked the bucket. Necklaces, rings and bracelets worth seventeen hundred quid. That begs two questions, Knight. Number one, why the sodding hell didn't the daft bugger nick it? Number two, where in the name of all that is holy did a part-time shop assistant get the cash to buy seventeen hundred quid's worth of jewellery?'

'I don't know,' Wendy replied. 'They might have been presents.'

'Who from, the Sultan of sodding Brunei? No, Knight, there's more to this girl than meets the eye and I'm going to find out what it is.'

With Culverhouse having a bee in his bonnet and being determined to act on it, Wendy decided she'd try and spend the rest of the day catching up on the paperwork related to the case. Each hour, the pile of papers on her desk grew. Logs of phone calls from cranks who'd rung in with their latest theory on who'd done it, records of local vagrants who'd turned up at the station and admitted to the murders to get a warm bed for the night; they were all there. A complete waste of everybody's time, but everything had to be logged and filed, just in case.

The only thing that kept her sane throughout the day was the thought that she'd be spending that night at Robert's.

Wendy shrieked with delight as the sun rose on Mildenheath the next morning. The sofa springs heaved underneath her as she thrust her pelvis back and forth. It felt amazing. Warm and soft, just divine. Robert grinned at Wendy as he held the two warm, juicy buns in his hands.

'Hot cross bun?' he said.

'Ooh, yes please. I was just thinking how soft and bouncy your sofa is while you were in the kitchen. I must get a new one myself.'

'It's very comfortable. In fact, I'll let you in on a little secret. I bought the softest and most comfortable sofa in the shop because I knew I'd keep falling asleep in it and then could justify buying myself a dedicated reading chair,' he said, pointing to the reclining leather armchair in the corner of the room.

'Why did you need to justify it to yourself?'

'Ah, lack of willpower, I guess.'

'I noticed you have a lot of books. You read much?' Wendy asked.

'As much as I can. The pen is mightier than the sword, as they say.'

'Indeed. I guess we should think ourselves lucky that the serial killer isn't killing people with pens,' Wendy joked.

'He used a sword?'

'Well, no, a knife, but you get the point.'

Robert switched the television on. A short, blonde-haired reporter was stood outside Mildenheath police station.

'Ooh, fame at last!' Robert joked.

'This latest murder,' the blonde-haired reporter explained, 'is thought to be linked with two others in Mildenheath which occurred over the last few days. Specific information from Mildenheath Police has been scarce with no word as to how these three young women came to meet their deaths. Their identities, however, were confirmed earlier this evening as twenty-one-year-old Ella Barrington, twenty-nine-year-old Maria Preston and seventeen-year-old Nicole Bryant. Local sources have confirmed that both Ella Barrington and Maria Preston were known prostitutes operating in the area but it is thought that Nicole Bryant was not working as a prostitute at the time of her death. Nonetheless, it appears that this is a line of enquiry which Mildenheath Police are following up.'

Before the reporter could finish her report, Robert got up and switched the TV off.

'Robert? What's that all about?' Wendy asked, confused.

'Well, it's not very nice is it? Having to hear about those people dying. No, I suspect you have enough of it at work. Would you like a cup of tea?'

'No, I'd like to know why you switched the TV off.'

'I told you. I didn't think you'd want to concentrate on work stuff outside of the office. Besides, I don't like hearing about serial killings. It gives me the creeps.'

'You seemed quite interested the other night.'

'Well, just taking a friendly interest, you know.'

The silence hung over the pair for a good two or three minutes before Robert, seemingly continuing a train of thought out loud, broke the deadlock.

'I read a book about something similar once,' Robert said. 'Turned out the father of the first victim had been the killer and had got such a buzz out of it that he just carried on killing women that reminded him of his daughter. Well, I'm just saying that it's not a massive leap of faith to have it work the other way round.'

'It's unlikely that Mr Bryant will have killed two random prostitutes and popped off his daughter as a *piece de resistance*, don't you think?' Wendy said. 'I think you've been reading too many books.'

'I see. Well, yes, I do read quite a lot. Quite a varied range of interests, I'm afraid, so I tend to buy a lot of books on various subjects.'

Wendy scanned the bookcase and her eyes rested on a section of eight or nine books on knots.

'You have a lot of books about knots,' Wendy said.

'Hmmm? Oh, yes. I... I was in the boy scouts. Sort of a long-running interest of mine. Never know when you might need to tie a proper knot.'

'Yes, I suppose there's a lot of call for them in accountancy practices in Mildenheath.'

'Well, not exactly, no. But I am quite keen on camping. I tend to refer to them for that.'

'You're going camping in October?' Wendy asked.

'No, why?'

'You've got two books on camping knots open on your coffee table. I just wondered why you were referring to them in the middle of October.'

'Oh, I just wanted to check something. A friend asked me to find something out about bowline knots for him. Think he's into fishing or something. Anyway, what's wrong with camping in October? It's still very warm at the moment.'

'Yeah.'

The words of Steve Wing and Frank Vine echoed through Wendy's head.

...each of the victims was found with a length of rope tied around their necks...they weren't your usual knots...Bowline knots... pretty handy for nooses...

A shiver ran down Wendy's spine. Did she believe in coincidences? At this moment she wasn't entirely sure. She made her excuses and left.

17

THERE WAS NO EASY WAY TO APPROACH THE SITUATION. Wendy was torn between her loyalty to the intuition she knew she had, and which had never failed her, and the overwhelming evidence before her.

'DS Knight, will you get to the sodding point?' Culverhouse asked, his patience wearing thin. 'What does a saucy date with some tart of an accountant have to do with my bloody murder investigation?'

'I think there might be a link somewhere, guv.'

'Well I'd be a very happy bunny if you'd cut the crap and tell me what it is. I've got to meet the Chief Constable at ten, and I've not had my breakfast yet.'

'This might sound a bit weird.'

'From what you've told me so far, I've had more sensible dreams after seven pints of lager and a chicken vindaloo.'

'I wouldn't bring it up if I didn't think it was important, guv. At first I didn't really notice anything. It's only in retrospect that things seem a little odd. Robert's been quite keen to find out more about the case every time we've met. I thought it was just natural curiosity at first but now I'm not so sure. He keeps asking about details, as if he's trying to find out how much we know. Then last night I was in his flat and I noticed he had a few books on knots in his bookcase. He said he had been a member of the boy scouts.'

'Ah, well, that's it then. Got him hook, line and sinker. I'll get DS Wing on the blues-and-twos down to the local scout hut to nick the lot of them. Perhaps we can do 'em for singing ging-gang-sodding-goolie in a public place. What in the name if *bloody hell* are you trying to say, Knight?'

'Guv, please give me a chance to explain. There were two books open on the coffee table. They were both open on pages about bowline knots.'

'Bowline knots?' Culverhouse asked, exasperated.

'Yes. The knot used to tie the ligatures in all three of the killings.'

'I see. Well, as you said, he's taking an interest. He probably looked it up to find out more about it after you told him about it.'

'Guv, I never mentioned bowline knots to Robert. Or anyone, for that matter. Hell, I haven't even mentioned rope or strangulation!'

'Has there been anything in the papers about it?'

'No, you told us not to mention anything related to the killing methods for fear of copycat killings.'

'I see. So there's no way this Ludford fellow could know that the murders were committed with this particular type of knot?'

'Well, so far as I can see there is only one way.'

'We can't jump to conclusions, Knight. There's every chance it could just be a coincidence. It's certainly a strong lead. Tell me, how did you meet Ludford?'

'He approached me outside a pub.'

'He approached you?'

'Yes.' She deigned not to tell Culverhouse that she had reversed into Ludford's car after a skinful of whisky.

'Right. This is all sounding a bit suss to me. I want you to keep seeing Ludford. Get more involved with him. It could be a vital way of obtaining information and closing the net in on him.'

'You think it could be him?'

'I've no idea, but it's strong enough to look into.'

'And you want me to get more involved? With a potential serial killer?'

'No, Knight, I want you to break off all contact, obtain no more information and leave him free to kill a load more girls. What do you bloody well think? Tell me, what are our options, exactly?'

'Well, when you put it like that...'

'Good. I want regular reports immediately after each meeting. I want everything recorded on tape. We'll get you fitted with a recording device.'

'Are you sure the Chief Constable will authorise that, guv?'

Culverhouse pulled a miniature clip-on microphone and hand-held digital recording unit from his desk drawer and placed it in front of Wendy.

'Sod the Chief Constable. I'll sort that out later. Consider it authorised.'

18

Wendy's head pounded as she tried to comprehend the situation. Over dinner that night her taste for red wine returned as, somehow, she and Michael managed to demolish two bottles between them.

She had found it difficult to know how to approach the situation, but she knew that somehow she needed to put her mind at rest.

'Did you find anything odd about Robert, Michael?'

'Odd? No, why? You gone off him already?'

'Not exactly, no. I just have one or two concerns.'

'About what? Don't tell me. He wears Y-fronts. Farts in bed? Picks his nose? Honestly, Wend. No-one's perfect. You've got to realise that you can't just keep discarding people over silly little things.'

'No, nothing like that. I'm worried that... Oh, don't worry. It's silly,' she replied, waving the conversation away.

'Come on, Wend. If you can't confide in me, who can you confide in? Remember what we said? We've both got to be completely open and honest with each other. It's the only way to strengthen the relationship again.'

Wendy sighed. 'You have to promise that you won't tell a single soul, Michael. I mean it. I could lose my job over it.'

'Your job? Wow, you think Robert is involved with some sort of illegal activity? Got to watch those accountants, you know!' What is it? Tax evasion? Cooking the books? Inflicting paper cuts with malice?'

'It's not funny, Michael. Listen. Those three girls were all killed in a very particular way. They were strangled with ropes. Not the same rope each time, but the same very specific knot. It's known as a bowline knot. It sounds stupid saying it now but Robert has a number of books on knots and I found two of them open on pages about bowline knots when I was at his house last night. He claimed it was something to do with a favour for a friend but I don't know. Now I think about it, he's been taking a very keen interest in the case and has been asking a lot of odd questions. I don't know why, but something doesn't quite seem right.'

Michael sat in silence for a few moments. 'And you think he could be the killer?'

'I don't want to think that.'

'But you do think it?'

'Oh, I don't know what I think right now. All I know is that I'm in a very sticky situation to say the least.'

Later that night, as Wendy tried to drift off to sleep, recurring visions kept flashing in front of her eyes. First the face of Ella Barrington, then Robert's books. Then Maria Preston, then the books. Then Nicole Bryant. Then the books. How could she have been so foolish? *I should have spotted the signs earlier*, she surmised. *Some detective.* Her heart juddered as a sudden thought entered her mind. What if Ludford had intended her to be the next victim? What if that was *still* his intention? What if he was completely mad? How could Culverhouse insist that she carry on seeing a potential serial killer? Was *he* mad? Or was *she* mad for thinking that a completely innocent man, the first man she'd let get close to her in years, was a serial killer? As she tried to comprehend her thoughts, the phone rang.

'Yes?' she said, picking it up.

'Culverhouse here. Listen, Knight. We've got a bit of a problem on our hands now. There's been a fourth murder.'

19

The lack of sleep didn't help Wendy one bit as she walked into the incident room late that night to meet with Culverhouse in the light of the latest killing.

'Sorry, Knight,' Culverhouse said, his hands raised, palms outward in mock apology on seeing her face. 'Unfortunately people aren't considerate enough to wait until daylight to get murdered.'

'Is it fresh?'

'No, she was killed the night before last. The pathologist reckons it was between seven in the evening and three in the morning. Rigor mortis already set in, yadda-yadda. Pathology have got the details.'

'Do we have a positive ID?'

'We do. Another easy one. It's starting to look like the killer *wants* these girls to be identified but I can't figure out for the life of me why. Grace Norris, an eighteen-year-old college student. A devout Catholic and local church volunteer. On the plus side, another Bible basher off our streets. On the other hand, bang goes my prossie theory.'

'So you're finally accepting that Nicole Bryant wasn't a prostitute?' Wendy asked, smiling.

'No, I'm accepting that Grace Norris wasn't a prostitute.'

Wendy sighed and shook her head. 'Definitely the same MO?'

'Without a shadow of a doubt,' Culverhouse replied. 'Absolutely identical.'

'So what the hell *does* link these women?'

'If I knew that, Knight, I wouldn't be farting about here at three o'clock in the bastard morning. I'd be tucked up in my jim-jams with a mug of Horlicks.'

Tell me about it, she wanted to say.

'Oh, but SOCO said there was one slight deviation from the MO,' he added.

'Right. So not absolutely identical after all?'

'Oh no, it was absolutely identical all right. But this time he raped her.'

'*Raped* her? He's not raped them before,' Wendy said, surprised.

'I know that, Knight. Hence the slight deviation.'

'But why now?'

'It looks as though he's stepping up his game. We've got some sort of cat and mouse game on our hands.'

'Did SOCO say whether intercourse occurred pre- or post-mortem?'

'If you mean did the bastard shag her when she was dead, we don't know yet. We're still waiting for forensics to get their turkey basters out.'

They sat down and examined the profiles of each victim, one by one. Their photographs were laid out on the table in front of them, a joyful family photo juxtaposed with the anguished death mask of each woman. Each letter of each of their names struck fear and anger into Wendy's gut.

ELLA BARRINGTON
MARIA PRESTON
NICOLE BRYANT
GRACE NORRIS

So their names were getting shorter. Ella Barrington: fourteen letters. Maria Preston: twelve letters. Nicole Bryant: twelve letters. Grace Norris: eleven letters. Would the next victim's name have ten letters in it? Would he finally stop killing once he'd found someone with a two-letter name? Wendy told herself this was a ridiculous theory and cursed her lack of sleep.

As the minutes and hours ticked by, conversation returned to Robert Ludford.

'Guv, I'm really not sure about this whole idea of getting involved with him. If he really is the murderer, he's stepped up his game big time with this one. I really don't think it's safe.'

'What other option do we have, Knight? We can't barge in and arrest him or search his house because the only evidence we have on him is that he once read a book on a similar type of knot that was used in the murders. Even that is circumstantial, but not circumstantial enough to be ignored. No, we can't do anything else but watch and observe him. Conventional surveillance would be useless, especially as you and he are already close and he seems to want to confide in you and speak to you about the case.'

'What if he's just after information?'

'Then we'll feed him red herrings. We'll soon find out if he's linked then.'

'I don't know, guv. I still don't feel safe.'

'You're a police officer, Knight,' Culverhouse said, lifting his coffee mug to his lips and taking a slurp before banging it back down on his desk. 'You're not meant to feel safe. Case closed.'

20

It was Tuesday evening when Wendy finally summoned up the courage to visit Robert Ludford's flat. The recording equipment tucked safely in her bag, the microphone clipped snugly inside the flap, she pressed the doorbell and waited for him to come to the door.

When he did, he seemed to immediately register Wendy's unease. Perhaps he was expecting it, she thought. What if he was onto her?

'Everything OK, sweetheart?' he said, placing his hand on her shoulder.

'Yes, sorry. Absolutely fine. Stressful day at work.'

'Ah, the murders?'

'Yes. There's been another victim.'

'Oh?' Robert said, seeming genuinely surprised.

'But I can't really talk about it. Can I come in? It's freezing out here.'

'Oh yes, of course. Sorry. Do come in. I'll put the kettle on.'

Settling on the armchair in the corner of the living room, Wendy felt this was the best spot to sit in, in order to get a good view of the whole room. If Ludford really was as dangerous as he seemed, she didn't want to leave anything to chance. She loosened the locks on the window behind her, saving herself a few valuable seconds should she need to make a quick escape.

'What are you doing?'

Wendy jumped. 'Robert! Oh, sorry. Nothing.'

'Were you trying to open the window?'

'No. Erm... yes. I'm a bit hot.'

'You were freezing cold not twenty seconds ago.'

'I know. That time of the month, you know.' The line guaranteed to stop any conversation with a male dead in its tracks.

'Oh, OK. Er, do you want sugar?'

Wendy remembered her mother and aunt giving her lots of old wives' tales and practical remedies for alleviating the symptoms of the menstrual cycle, but she didn't recall sugar being one.

'In your tea,' he explained. 'Do you want sugar?'

'Oh. Yes, one please.'

Wendy watched closely as Ludford returned to the kitchen. Not wanting to leave her seat for fear of him catching her mid-snoop yet again, Wendy scanned the room from her padded lookout post. As her crooked head guided her eyes along the spines of Ludford's books, she was jolted back upright by the ringing of a phone. She heard him answer.

'Hello? Ah, Nigel! I've been meaning to…' Ludford's words trailed off as he kicked the door closed. The satisfying click of the latch in its socket triggered a sigh from Wendy. Realising that this was her chance, she jumped from her seat and skipped over to the side dresser, whereupon she started rifling through the drawers in search of any incriminating evidence.

She knew she was looking for something which would either prove or disprove – she still wasn't quite sure which — the theory that Ludford was involved with the serial killings, but she hadn't quite bargained on what stared back at her from the third drawer down on the left. Half of it glistened silver under the angle-poise lamp, the other half glued to a filthy napkin with a dark reddish-brown dried adhesive. Of course, Wendy knew exactly what was staring back at her. You didn't become a DS without knowing a bloodstained knife when you saw one.

Skipping back across the room, she grabbed her handbag, extracted a handkerchief of her own from within it and wrapped the soiled knife and attached handkerchief carefully, being careful not to make direct contact with it, before placing it in her bag and quietly closing the drawer.

The rules of all good thriller films dictated that Ludford would walk through the door at that moment. In reality, it seemed like an age. Wendy sat back in her now-useless lookout spot, desperate to launch herself through the half-open window and run back home through the streets. Doing so would alarm Ludford and he'd soon find out she had the knife. Then who would be his next victim? No, it was too risky. She would have to sit it out and wait for him to come back into the room before making her excuses and leaving.

When the age finally passed and Ludford returned to the living room, he froze on the spot.

'Jesus, Wendy. You look like you've seen a ghost. Are you all right?'

'I think... I don't really feel very well, actually.'

'Oh. You must be coming down with a fever. That must be why you wanted the window open all of a sudden. Here, let me take your temperature.'

Ludford walked over to Wendy to place his hand on her forehead.

'No! I mean... I'm sure I'll be fine. I just need to go home and rest.'

'OK, leave your car here and I'll give you a lift back.'

'No, no. It's fine. I'm only round the corner. Please, I'll drive.'

'Are you sure? You look terrible.'

'I'll be fine.'

Locking the car door immediately, Wendy started the car and headed straight for the station.

21

WENDY STRUGGLED TO GET HER BREAKFAST DOWN. ASIDE from the deep, nauseous feeling in the pit of her stomach, she supposed that if she managed to eat she'd have even more of a struggle trying to *keep* it down.

'You OK, Wend? You look a little... shaken.'

'I'm fine, Michael. Honestly.'

'You sure? You were at Robert's last night, weren't you?'

The name sent shivers down Wendy's spine.

'Yes. Yes, I was.'

'Did anything happen? Be honest with me, Wend. You look terrible.'

'Will you stop telling me how bad I look? I fucking *feel* terrible. Look, I'm in a situation which I *really* don't want to be in,' she said, stirring her cereal with her spoon.

'What kind of situation? With Robert?'

'Yes, with Robert.'

'Tell me, Wend. Be honest. Did he hurt you?'

'Michael. If I tell you, you have to swear absolute secrecy. This is bigger than you could ever know and it is absolutely imperative that you do not breathe a word to a living soul. Do you understand?'

'It goes without saying, Wend. I just want to know what's happened.'

'Culverhouse... I... we, both think Robert Ludford may have something to do with the deaths that have occurred recently.'

'What, you mean he knew the girls?'

'I don't know. I think he knew one of them, at least. He went rather odd at the mention of Nicole Bryant on the TV the other night and now refuses to talk about the situation. Listen, Michael, we think he may have been *directly* involved.'

'Directly? You mean he killed them?' Michael said, his eyes wide in shock.

'We can't be sure, but the clues are getting stronger. You remember I told you about the knots? Well, I... I found something in his flat last night.'

'Oooh, not another book?' Michael said, sarcastically.

'No. A blood-stained knife,' Wendy said, her eyes finally meeting Michael's for the first time that morning.

'Woah. OK, this is serious.'

'Exactly. I took it straight to the station last night. Forensics are working on it as we speak. We should know later today whether the blood matches that of any of the victims.'

'And if it does?'

'If it does, we have a real problem.'

Wendy felt all eyes on her as she walked through the police station later that morning. The overnight desk sergeant had clearly blabbed everything about the knife to her colleagues last night. *Stupid bitch. Never trust a desk sergeant.*

Walking into the incident room, the eyes seemed to sharpen and focus on her even more tightly. *Good news travels fast.* Wendy could almost read their minds. *Stupid cow, getting involved with a serial killer. How could she not have known? Some bloody cop she is. Couldn't even spot a serial killer in her own bed, the cheap slut.*

'Guv. I presume you're aware of last night's development,' Wendy said confidently, trying to ignore the eyes of her colleagues.

'I think the King of sodding Spain is aware of last night's development, Knight. What in the name of hell were you playing at, giving a potential murder weapon to a part-time desk sergeant? You're fucking CID, for Christ's sake. I suppose you'll be filing your confidential reports with the caretaker next?'

'I'm sorry, guv,' Wendy explained, shuffling her feet. 'I panicked.'

'You panicked? Fat fucking lot of good panicking at a blood-stained knife does when you're meant to be investigating a murder!'

'With respect, guv, it's a little bit different this time.'

'You're damn right it's a little bit different this time. This time you've been shagging the prime suspect!'

'I didn't know he was a suspect at the time, guv,' she said quietly. 'And we didn't *shag*.'

'You didn't shag? Well what the bloody hell do you call it then?'

'We made love.'

The incident room tittered like a group of schoolchildren in a sex education class. Culverhouse's glowering eyes ensured it ceased as soon as it had started.

'Right. Well, whatever you want to bloody well call it, the fact of the matter is you've got some serious explaining to do to Chief Constable Hawes if it turns out that one speck of one victim's blood is on that knife. He already has my head on the chopping block and I will *not* allow your fucking bungee knickers to have me kicked off the case. Do you understand?'

'Yes, guv,' she said sullenly.

'Good. Next door. Everyone. Morning briefing.'

Wendy took in very little of that morning's briefing as her mind kept replaying the moment she found the knife in Ludford's drawer. Now she felt anxious and nervous at what the future held. Her career was in jeopardy and she knew it. She supposed it didn't matter too much that she didn't take in a word of the briefing. Of course, she knew the whole story better than anyone. All the pieces were starting to come together. The seemingly random meeting in the car park, the books on knots, the evasive tone regarding Nicole Bryant and, of course, the knife.

After the briefing, Wendy followed Culverhouse back into the incident room. A woman from the forensics lab was waiting for him. Culverhouse and the woman went into his office and closed the door. A few minutes later, the door opened and the woman from forensics left. As Wendy moved towards the door, it opened further and Culverhouse came into view. A lock of hair hung over his forehead, hooked into the creases that now appeared on his brow. Wendy knew exactly what had been said.

'Wh... who... whose blood?'

'Grace Norris. It's the murder weapon. Ludford is our killer.'

22

WENDY HAD FINALLY MANAGED TO CONVINCE CULVER-house that if he must arrest Robert Ludford at work, he should have him called to reception and do it there rather than cause a scene in front of the whole office. Reluctantly, he had agreed.

The girl at the reception desk seemed chirpier than she should have been. Culverhouse wasn't entirely sure who she was talking to, what with the headset she was wearing to answer the phones.

'Mr Ludford? Yes, I can call him for you. Do you have an appointment?'

'We don't need an appointment, love,' Culverhouse said.

'Well, is he expecting you?' the receptionist said with a professional smile.

'I should imagine so, yes.'

'Right. Well, I can certainly call him and ask if he's free. Would you like to hold on for a moment?'

'Delighted,' Culverhouse said.

The young, blonde-haired receptionist picked up the phone and dialled Ludford's extension.

'Hello, Mr Ludford? I've got a gentlemen and a lady here who say you're expecting them. Oh, I see.' She turned to Culverhouse. 'He says he isn't expecting any visitors today. What did you say your name was again?'

'I didn't,' Culverhouse replied. 'Tell him Wendy Knight is here.'

'Oh, OK. He says the young lady with him is a Wendy Knight, Mr Ludford. Does that mean anything to you? OK, yes, I'll let them know.' She put the phone down. 'Mr Ludford will be down in a few moments, if you'd like to take a seat.'

Don't worry about us, darling, we'll do this standing up. You've got front-row tickets.'

When Ludford finally emerged from the lift a minute or two later, he smiled at Wendy before noticing the man who was with her.

'Hello, Wendy. What a lovely surprise. Colleague of yours?'

'Yes, Robert. This is a colleague of mine. Listen, I'm sorry for—'

'Right, Ludford. You're nicked,' Culverhouse interjected. Ludford let out a nervous laugh. 'Sorry – I'm *what?*'

Wendy's head dropped as Culverhouse placed the handcuffs on Ludford.

'You heard. I'm arresting you on suspicion of the murder of Grace Norris. You do not have to say anything, but it may harm your defence if you do not mention when questioned something which you later rely on in court. Anything you do say may be given in evidence.'

'Murder?! Please tell me this is some sort of joke. I've never even heard of Grace Norris! Wendy? What's going on?' Robert's features conveyed a mixture of surprise and disappointment.

'I'm sorry, Robert.'

Ludford's face was a picture of sterile depression as he sat, head bowed, in the police station's interview room.

'This interview will commence at exactly fourteen hundred hours. Present are myself, DCI Jack Culverhouse, DS Wendy Knight and the suspect, Mr Robert Ludford. Mr Ludford, are you familiar with the name Grace Norris?'

'I already told you this,' Ludford replied.

'For the benefit of the tape, Mr Ludford.'

'No. I had never heard of Grace Norris until my arrest earlier this afternoon.'

'I am now presenting the suspect with exhibit one. Mr Ludford, do you recognise this object?'

Culverhouse placed the knife and handkerchief, sealed inside a zip-lock bag, onto the desk.

'It's a knife,' Ludford replied.

'Yes. Is it your knife?'

'No, I don't think so.'

'You don't think so?' Culverhouse said.

'I have a lot of knives for camping and cooking. I don't remember the aesthetics of each one.'

'Let me be more specific,' Culverhouse said. 'Did you use this knife to kill Grace Norris?'

'No! I haven't killed anyone!'

'Mr Ludford, this knife was found in a drawer in your flat. The blood on it belongs to Grace Norris.'

But... that's not possible! Wait. What do you mean it was found in my flat? You haven't searched my flat.'

'Its discovery was incidental, Mr Ludford.'

Wendy shuffled uncomfortably.

'Incidental? You mean... Wendy? Did you have something to do with this?'

Wendy remained silent. Culverhouse slowly rose to his feet and cleared his throat.

'DS Knight, can I have a word with you outside for a moment?' He walked towards the door and turned back towards the tape machine. '14:02. DCI Culverhouse and DS Knight have left the room.'

Wendy could still not lift her head as they stood outside the interview room.

'Now, you listen to me, Knight. You insisted on being in on this interview knowing damn well that you shouldn't be within five miles of this police station right now. The least you can do is co-operate with the bloody case, do you hear?'

'It's awkward, guv,' Wendy said.

'I know it's awkward, Knight. Serial killers aren't exactly fluffy bastard bunnies. I want professionalism and cooperation or I want you out, got it?'

Wendy nodded sullenly. 'Got it.'

As they re-entered the room, Culverhouse barked his commentary back at the tape.

'Wendy? Is it true?' Robert asked. 'Did you find this knife in my house?'

Wendy was silent for a few moments before speaking. 'Yes.'

'But... how?'

Culverhouse interrupted. 'Because you didn't hide it very well, Mr Ludford.'

'I didn't hide it at all! It wasn't me!' he shouted.

'Do you live alone, Mr Ludford?' Culverhouse asked.

'Well, yes.'

'Then who do you suppose put it there?'

Ludford appeared to think hard. 'Well, no-one could have. I don't even really have visitors. That is, apart from Wendy.'

'For the benefit of the tape, Mr Ludford is referring to DS Knight. The particulars are covered within the case file. Mr Ludford, let me get this right. You form a relationship with a police officer in order to find out information about how close they are to finding out that you're going around killing young, innocent women. You ensure that she's the only other person allowed in your flat so when you're finally caught you can claim she's fitted you up. Am I starting to get somewhere close to the truth?'

'No! None of that is true at all!'

'Tell me about the knots, Ludford,' Culverhouse said, not leaving a moment's silence.

'The knots?'

'The knots.'

Wendy's confidence had returned. 'When I was at your flat you had two books open on the coffee table in your living room detailing the specific types of knot which were used to kill each of the murdered girls.'

'I… I told you why I had those books open,' Ludford said.

'For the benefit of the tape, Mr Ludford told me he was looking something up for a friend.'

'Yes. That's right.'

'Which friend?' Culverhouse asked.

'I can't say.'

'We can always add obstruction of justice to your growing list of charges, if you wish.'

'All right, all right. It was an old Army friend of mine.'

'Army friend?' Wendy said. 'You never told me you were in the Army.'

Culverhouse interrupted again. 'Why did you leave the Army, Mr Ludford?'

Robert Ludford let out a loud laugh, his shoulders bouncing rhythmically. 'You wouldn't believe me if I told you.'

'Try me,' Culverhouse said.

'I got sick of death.'

'If you'll forgive me, Mr Ludford, all the evidence points to the contrary. What was your friend's name?'

'Geoff Casey.'

'And where does Mr Casey live?'

'In a town called Woodend.'

'Would you care to enlighten us as to where that is?'

'Just outside Christchurch.'

'Christchurch in New Zealand?'

'Yes, Inspector. There's no way Geoff Casey is your murderer, if that's what you're thinking. As unlikely as it sounds, it's a horrible coincidence. Bowline knots aren't exactly rare, but Geoff remembered that I was quite adept with them during our Army days and asked me how to tie one. He lives near the coast and had landed himself a day's sailing with a potential lady friend. He's the same silly old sod he always used to be. Didn't have a clue how to tie a bowline knot, never mind how to steer the boat. I couldn't help him with that bit, of course.'

'An admirable story, Mr Ludford. Do you have one for how the blood-stained murder weapon miraculously appeared in your drawer yet?'

'No,' Ludford said sullenly.

'Well that's a shame. For you, at least.'

Wendy spoke up. 'How about your reaction to the mention of Nicole Bryant on the television the other night? You wouldn't discuss her case at all, despite being quite interested in the other victims.'

'Some might say *too* interested,' Culverhouse said.

Ludford sighed heavily. 'This isn't going to look good at all, I'm afraid.'

'None of it's looking particularly good right now, Mr Ludford.'

'Look, I did something very bad and very foolish but I certainly didn't kill anyone. A couple of months before I met you, Wendy, I was approached by Nicole Bryant in a bar in town. She was there with a few friends and they were all pretty drunk. By the end of the night her friends had gone off and left her so I offered to walk her home to make sure she was safe and didn't get hurt. I didn't see any harm in it. When we got back to hers, she grabbed me on the doorstep and tried to kiss me. I pulled away and she told me she wanted to have sex. I told her I couldn't as I didn't know her and I had half a feeling she wasn't even an adult. The next day she was waiting for me when I got home from work. I have no idea how she found out where I lived. She told me that if I didn't give her £250 in cash, she'd go to the police and say I'd raped her. That isn't something someone in my profession can risk, and I just panicked. I gave her the cash and hoped she'd disappear. A few days later she sent me a page torn out of a jeweller's catalogue with a hideously expensive bracelet circled in black marker pen.'

'And you bought it for her?'

'Yes. I just wanted her to leave me alone. I couldn't risk her going to the police, even though I was innocent. I know what the law is like in cases like that and I couldn't risk it. I guess today just goes to prove it.'

'It proves nothing, Mr Ludford,' Culverhouse said. 'Why didn't you go to the police?'

'Look. I didn't know what to do. She kept blackmailing me, wanting more money and more expensive gifts.'

'So you decided to kill her?' Culverhouse asked.

'No! I haven't killed anybody!'

'So who did?'

'I don't know! I had mixed emotions when I heard that Nicole had been killed. On one hand, I hated her for what she did to me and how she was so prepared to ruin an innocent man's life and I was glad she was out of my way. On the other hand, of course, two parents just lost a daughter. You have to believe me, though. I did not kill Nicole Bryant.'

'And what about Grace Norris?'

'No! I haven't killed anyone, Inspector.'

As Ludford sat stewing in his cell, Wendy and Culverhouse planned their next move. Step one would have to be to ring Ludford's friend in New Zealand in order to confirm his story. As they were buried deep in thought, Culverhouse's phone rang.

'Yes? Ah-ha. Right. I see. And you're absolutely certain of that? Right. OK. No, no, that's fine. Thank you.'

Wendy cocked her head to the side and waited for Culverhouse to explain.

'That was forensics. They've checked the fingerprints on the knife.'

'And?'

'Ludford's aren't on it.'

The atmosphere in Ludford's cell seemed to have lifted when he heard what Culverhouse had to say to him.

'So I'm free to go, Inspector?'

'Not quite, no.'

'But I thought you said my fingerprints weren't on it?'

'They aren't. But that doesn't mean you weren't wearing gloves.'

'Oh, for heaven's sake! I've told you everything!'

'Besides, you still need to explain why the knife was found in your flat.'

'I've already told you! I don't know why! I didn't bloody put it there!'

'Listen, Ludford. Your prints not being on the knife doesn't get you out of trouble quite that easily. We've got a lot to pin on you so you've got some explaining to do if you want to wriggle out of this one. Now, where were you on the night Ella Barrington was killed?'

'Jesus, I don't know! I didn't exactly bring my diary down here with me, Inspector. All I know is that I haven't killed anyone. How can I prove that to you?'

'Well, you're going to need alibis for the dates of the murders, for a start, or it's not looking very good for you at all. Maybe we'll try a more recent one. Where were you on the night Grace Norris was killed?'

'Jesus... probably either at work or at home. I don't know. I'd have to check my diary. Probably at home, though. Work has been quiet recently.'

A sudden realisation hit Wendy. She knew *exactly* where Ludford had been the night Grace Norris was killed. *He had been with her!* It all came flooding back now. She kicked herself for being so reckless and not spotting it sooner but she had found herself so wrapped up in coming to terms with Ludford as a suspect that she... Shit! It couldn't be him!

'Guv, can I have a quick word outside, please?' Wendy said.

As they stepped outside the interview room, Wendy was quite unsure as to how Culverhouse would react to her new development. She was pretty sure she knew, though.

'Guv, I know where Ludford was the night Grace Norris was killed. I was at his flat. All evening.'

'You were at his flat? All evening? And you've only just bloody remembered this?'

'I'm sorry, guv. I got caught up in everything that was going on and I didn't realise the connection between the dates.'

'You're going to have to get used to being caught up in things going on if you want to make a CID copper, DS Knight. What time did you leave Ludford's that night?'

'I didn't. I was there until the morning.'

'And what time did you get there the night before?'

'About eight, I think.'

'Right. So that leaves an hour beforehand in which he could've killed her. That's if the pathologist was right. And you were with him all the time?'

'Yes.'

'How can you be sure he didn't leave the house during the night?'

'Let's just say we weren't exactly asleep.'

'Too much information, Knight. Too much fucking information.'

'You asked!'

'A simple "yes I'm sure" would have sufficed. So what does that prove anyway? Maybe he didn't kill Grace Norris, maybe he did. Maybe the pathologist got the times wrong. That doesn't mean he's clear of all the others. And if that's the case, it certainly doesn't mean that little slag Bryant is any less the hooker I always thought she was.'

'Guv! Listen to me! You know as well as I do that these murders were all carried out by the same person. Forensics have said as much. Nicole Bryant was not a prostitute and the same person who killed Grace Norris killed all the other girls too. And that person probably wasn't Robert Ludford.'

'Probably wasn't? I'm going to need more convincing than that, Knight.'

'For Christ's sake! Why do you always get a bee in your bonnet about these things? *Ludford is not the killer!* We can't keep him under arrest any longer without infringing what human rights the poor man has left.'

'You listen to me, DS Knight. I've been in the police force a bloody long time and I know when I'm right about something. Hell, I've not been wrong yet. My instinct is my biggest virtue and I'm telling you now that I am not letting that man go until I've pinned every single bloody one of those murders on him.'

At that moment, a young female Constable with long, blonde flowing hair jogged down the corridor towards them, being careful not to trip over in her short heels.

'DCI Culverhouse, we've had a call come through. There's been another murder. It's the same as all the others. Thing is, the guy reckons he saw a bloke running off from the scene about fifteen minutes ago. The body's still warm.'

Wendy glanced sideways at Culverhouse with a wry smile.

An hour later, the SOCO team had confirmed without a doubt that the new body had been dead no longer than an hour or two, thereby proving that Robert Ludford could not have been the killer — of that victim, at least. Wendy did not know what to feel. A torrid mix of private relief and elation mixed with professional anger and desperation washed over her.

The anger and desperation had spread elsewhere in Mildenheath, although the family of Barbara North could not be said to have experienced the relief and elation in tandem. Wendy sat and flicked through the manila file as she read the forensic report on Barbara, barely thirty-six years old, and the savage way in which her life had been cut short. She noted something rather odd about this one, though. The forensics report stated, quite clearly at the bottom of the third page: EARLOBES AND EXTERNAL EAR FLAPS NOT PRESENT. BITE MARKS APPARENT – CONFIRMED HUMAN. MISSING PIECES NOT PRESENT. *Jesus Christ! He'd bitten off and eaten her ears!* As she turned to the next page, the words burned into her eyes: NO TRAIL OF BLOOD APPARENT. MURDER AND REMOVAL OF EARS ASSUMED TO HAVE TAKEN PLACE AT THE SCENE. *He'd killed her and eaten her ears in broad daylight!* The very fact that the dog walker had found Barbara's body just after the murder had taken place went to show just what lengths the killer was now going to and what risks he was willing to take to ensure he got away with murder.

23

Wendy collapsed with hysterical sobs as Michael comforted her. Her body heaved under the pressure of her rhythmic convulsions as she tried to explain the source of her desperation.

'It's OK, Wend. Just calm down and catch your breath. Then you can try and tell me what's wrong.'

Wendy took a few moments until she was sure she could speak without interjecting with squeaks and Michael Jackson-esque yowls.

'It... it isn't Robert. He's not the killer, Michael. He can't be.'

'He's not? Wow. Well, surely that must be a good thing, then.'

'It is! It is!'

'So what's the matter, Wend?' Michael's old self had come out in a way that almost took Wendy by surprise. She couldn't remember how long it had been since she had seen his true and caring personality, not under the influence of narcotics.

'Now we're back at square one. We have no idea who the killer is or where to even start looking. There's no pattern whatsoever other than the way they were killed and he's killing more and more often. All this rests on my shoulders and my stupid idea that Robert might have been involved. If it wasn't for me, we might have caught the killer earlier and saved Barbara North from being killed.'

'But you said yourself that you had no idea who it might have been other than Robert so you would have been no further along if you hadn't arrested him, surely?'

'It's wasted time, Michael. And we don't have any time to waste!'

'So if the Barbara North one wasn't him, that doesn't mean he didn't do the others, does it? What about a gang doing them?'

'Unlikely,' Wendy replied.

'Surely Culverhouse has got an idea up his sleeve? He's always so cock-sure he knows exactly what he's doing.'

'All we have at the moment is the witness.'

'Witness?' Michael asked.

'Yeah. The guy who found Barbara North's body reckons he saw a man running away from the scene.'

'Did he get a good description?'

'No, he just saw him in shadow. Couldn't even tell us his height or what he was wearing, but we're working on him. Hopefully we'll be able to get some sort of vague description and work from that.'

'Was there any CCTV?'

'Usual story. It was facing the other way.'

'And what about the knife in Robert's drawer? How was that explained?'

'I don't know. He reckons he doesn't know of anyone who'd have a grudge against him. He reckons he's going to go to a hypnotist to try and access his "innermost thoughts" and come up with some names for us to pursue.'

'Wow. Bit of a stab in the dark, then.'

'This is no time for puns, Michael.'

'Heh. I'm sorry, I didn't mean it. I didn't even realise until after I'd said it. Listen, I'll run you a nice hot bath with that lavender oil, OK? I want you to spend the evening in there relaxing and forgetting all about this case until the morning. You're not going to get anywhere without a clear head. All right?'

'All right. And Michael?'

'Mmmm?'

'Thank you. Thank you for being there.'

'You were there for me too, Wend. Just paying back the favour,' Michael said, smiling.

Little more than an hour later, the lilting scent of laven-der wafted through the air as Wendy sunk her shoulders back into the warm water. She let out an almighty sigh from a breath she didn't even remember taking in and tried to think just how long she had been holding on to this tension. Michael was right: she'd relax and de-stress as much as she could and go back to work tomorrow with a clear head; the clear head which was needed if she was going to finally make tracks and stop the killer ending more innocent lives.

As she began to drift off to sleep, she was woken by the ringing of her mobile phone.

'God, damn it!' Fumbling her hand along the bathmat, she finally found it and slid her finger across the screen to activate the call.

'Robert? What is it? I'm in the bath.'

'I… I need to see you, Wendy,' Robert said, his voice far more serious than she'd ever heard it before.

'What's up, Robert? You sound edgy.'

'Wendy, will you come over, please? I need to talk to you about something.'

'Robert, it's quarter-to-eleven. Can't we talk on the phone?'

'I need your help, Wendy. It's important. Please… please just come.'

'Yes, OK. I'll be right over. Just wait for me.'

With that, Wendy hauled herself out of the bath, regained her exhaled tension and dried herself off before throwing on some clothes.

'Got to nip out, Michael. Back soon!' she shouted towards her brother's bedroom. Darting down the stairs, she threw on her shoes, grabbed her car keys and jogged to her car as she felt her wet hair soak through the back of her blouse.

Less than two minutes into her journey, her phone rang again. Without thinking, she pressed the button on her car radio and answered the call.

'Robert?'

'Almost, but sexier,' Culverhouse said.

'Oh, guv. What's up? I can't talk, I've got to be somewhere.'

'At this time of night?'

'It's a long story; and even I don't know what it is. Robert's asked me to come over. He said he needed to see me urgently.'

'Are you sure that's wise?'

'No, but I need to do it.'

'Right, well I think I should come with you,' he said. 'He's still not off the hook yet, and he's still a suspect.'

'Honestly guv, there's no need. I'll call you if anything happens.'

'Well I hope you're not going to be late or hungover tomorrow. I'll catch up with you in the morning.'

Wendy hung up the phone and continued the seemingly endless drive to Robert Ludford's house.

The house was eerily silent as Wendy's car coasted into the driveway. There were no lights on, no signs of life.

She switched off her car engine and made her way towards the building before reaching the front door. She went to ring the doorbell but something made her change her mind. Female instinct, perhaps. She tried the doorknob. The door opened. Inside, the lights all seemed to be switched off.

'Robert? Robert, it's me, Wendy.' She fumbled in the darkness as she made her way through the hallway and into the kitchen. She almost stumbled as she kicked something left carelessly in the middle of the floor. Cursing to herself, she made her way to the living room. As she entered the room, she felt the presence of another person. *Robert must be in here.* As she switched on the light, she saw exactly who it was.

24

Wendy stood, surprised but unsure what to make of the situation.

'Michael? What are you doing here? Where's Robert? He called me a few minutes ago. He sounded panicked. I don't know what's going on, Michael.'

'Oh, there's a lot you don't know, Wend. I'm afraid Robert can't be here right now, so you'll have to make do with me.'

'What's going on, Michael?'

'Oh, come on, Wend! Surely you must have worked it out by now! You and the great Magnifico down at the precious station! But, just in case you haven't...'

The force of Michael's fist jarred Wendy's head back, smashing the glass pane of the photograph which hung on the wall behind her.

As far as she was concerned she had only blinked, yet suddenly she found herself sat in Robert Ludford's kitchen, her hands and legs tied to a wooden chair.

'Nice of you to rejoin us, Wend. As I was saying... Just in case you haven't worked it out yet, I've brought along a few clues. Buzz in when you think you know the answer! I give you, DS Knight, exhibit one!' With a flourish, Michael pulled a pair of gloves from the inside of his jacket pocket. 'A little bit bloodstained, I grant you, but an excellent clue nonetheless. Still no closer to the answer? Let's try exhibit two!' With the grace of a game-show host and the subtlety of a brick, Michael pulled a length of rope from the other jacket pocket. 'Now, the eagle-eyed amongst you will have noticed that this is the same rope that you are tied to that chair with. Not only that, but it's tied with a couple of very handy bowline knots. The same rope, too, that was involved with one or two murders which I believe you have been investigating. Is any of this starting to ring a bell, Wend?'

Wendy nodded, cautiously, trying to judge Michael's next move. She felt strangely calm.

'Now, I would have had an exhibit three but unfortunately someone seems to have a certain bloodstained knife in their custody down at the police station. Never mind. I'll move straight on to this week's star prize!'

Wendy dared not avert her gaze from straight-ahead as Michael walked behind her chair and fumbled around on the floor before making his way back to his original vantage point in front of the door.

'Recognise *this*, Wend?'

Wendy screamed at the top of her lungs, the masking tape cutting into the sides of her mouth as her body rocked and convulsed at the gruesome sight of Robert Ludford's head swinging before her, dangling from the locks of hair that Michael had in his grasp, the cold, glassy eyes staring through her. The look of terror on Robert's face burnt itself into Wendy's vision.

'Say hello to your sweetheart!' Michael, his menacing grin turning into a vicious scowl, jumped forward and pushed his face and Ludford's death mask in front of Wendy. 'Do you want to fuck him now? Do you? I bet you do, you little slut! I bet you'd still fuck him even now! You're nothing but a cheap whore! The *ultimate* cheap whore!' Michael released his grip on the red, sticky hair and the bludgeoned head dropped to the floor with a sickening thud. A strange thought went through Wendy's mind: *Ouch, that'll bruise.*

'That's all you are, isn't it? Just another little slut. Just the same as you always have been. Oh yes, you're worse than the rest. You're ten times filthier than Barbara North and a thousand times filthier than Ella Barrington. Top-class prostitute, they called her! Fucking clueless piece of shit, more like. Now, that Barbara, she was a bit of a goer for an old bird. Filthy as you like. Had her on a recommendation, as it happens. I've a feeling, though, that my favourite is going to be you, Wendy. Oh yes. You're the next and final one. It's you and then it's me. The world will be rid of all its filth and all its sluts and I will die a hero, a martyr to the cause. Do you remember the boyfriends you used to bring home from school, Wend? Hell, I do. I remember every single one. I remember their names, I remember the dates. I remember the *bang-bang-banging* against the wall, the screams and moans coming from your filthy, slutty little gob and I prayed from that moment that every horrible little slag on this planet should pay the price. If they want other men to use them as objects of play and gratification, why not me? Why can I not do as I please? Well, I think you'll find I have. And now I'm going to die a happy man, Wend. I've done my bit. Almost, anyway.'

Laughing, Michael slung open the kitchen door, and waltzed up the stairs. A thousand thoughts flew round Wendy's mind but she was unable to see any of them for the one which pervaded all: *she was going to die.*

As he re-entered the room a few minutes later, Wendy's hysterical fits of sobbing had ceased and Michael's face seemed much calmer; resigned to what he would have to do. It was almost as though the post-interval curtain had just lifted on a whole new act of the play. She spoke just two words.

'Why, Michael?'

'Why? *Why?* Ho ho! That's a good one, Wend!' Deranged Michael was back. 'Who knows? Who truly knows? I may have my reasons, but does that mean I truly know? Maybe it was the long, drawn-out hell of a childhood that I put squarely on your shoulders.'

'I didn't bring you up, Michael.'

'No, you didn't, but you're the reason no-one else did. Mum and dad doted on you. Why was it always you who was destined to go far? Why was it you that dad had earmarked for the police force and me for your first nick? Speaking of which, maybe it was the fact that my own sister had me banged up!'

'I didn't have you banged up, Michael. I tried to help you kick your... your problem. All I did was try to help.'

'That's all you ever do, isn't it, Wend? *Try*. You don't know what trying is! My whole life I've spent trying to come to terms with the fact that no matter how hard I tried, no matter how hard I worked, I would always be nothing. Do you have any idea what that's like? Being tied back with an enormous elastic band? When no matter how hard you pull away, it recoils and pulls you back twice as hard? Why do you think I turned to smack in the first place, Wend? Just a bit bored, was I? No, Wendy, I was *fucked in the head*,' he said, jabbing his index finger into his right temple as he screamed into Wendy's face. 'Fucked in the head because of *you*.'

'That's no justification for killing those girls, Michael.' Wendy's voice sounded strangely calm, if a little grave.

'I don't *need* justification, Wendy. I have a *thousand* and one things going through my head right now, whizzing around inside. Do you have any idea? *Do you?*' Michael's frantic, throbbing temples were inches from Wendy's face now. 'No. You have no idea. I grew to resent every small piece of happiness you felt. You made me do that, Wend.

You pushed me to it. I never had parents. All right, so I lived in the same house as two people who fucked and gave birth to me, but I never had parents. I had to bring myself up, a child, knowing my slut whore sister was getting everything she wanted.'

'It wasn't like that, Michael! I don't know what is giving you these ideas but it's all totally wrong. You have some problems, Michael. We can talk about them. This can be sorted.'

'I have plenty of fucking problems, Wend! Six of them, to be precise! And I'm about to make it seven.'

'Michael, I..." Wendy's voice trailed off as she watched Michael slowly remove a length of rope from his pocket. It was tied in a bowline knot.

'Y'know, I gave the others all a chance to say goodbye. Only if they were good, like. That Nicole Bryant tried screaming instead and she got what she asked for. The others all played it very nicely and pleaded for their lives. Do you have any idea how powerful that makes me feel? I've never felt powerful before, Wend. It's addictive.'

Wendy sobbed. 'Michael…'

'Do you have any last words? Better make them good…'

Wendy paused and shook her head as a tear rolled from her eye. Through the salty kaleidoscope she could just make out Michael's face. It was smiling. As her body and mind fell short of any thought or feeling for the first time in her life, she realised it would also be the only time. No thoughts crossed her mind; no feeling flowed through her veins. Only the gentle rasp of the rope that passed around her neck and tightened. Tightened.

25

As LUCIDITY AND SENSITIVITY FLOWED BACK INTO HER, her only sense was that of a fading sensation; a totally different one to the physical indifference she had felt just moments ago. This time, she was slipping. Her chest heaved violently and gasped for air as her cells used up the last of their precious oxygen. She could feel her lungs burning, thrusting against the inside of her ribcage as they lunged desperately for an intake of that precious nectar. But none was forthcoming. As her vision faded to black via dancing stars, she felt a new kind of consciousness. As black faded back through dancing stars, the air flowed back into her lungs, which gasped and gulped, the burning sensation making her chest heave. She had heard no sound, except for the shrill piercing sound of tinnitus. Not, that is, until she looked up in the direction of where her killer had been stood.

'Fuck me, that was bloody lucky. Thought I'd got the wrong house for a minute.'

'Guv!' she choked, desperately looking around her, 'Where is he? Where's Michael?'

Culverhouse raised his hand to show Wendy the blood-spattered kettle, a head-shaped dent in the side of it.

'I don't think he'll be getting up for a while. Fancy a cuppa?'

'Not right now,' Wendy laughed, mostly out of relief. 'What made you come here? I said I would be fine.'

'And I said you wouldn't be. Was I wrong?'

'You never are, are you?' she said with gritted teeth.

'Bloody good job too, eh?'

26

THE CHEERS RANG OUT THROUGH THE INCIDENT ROOM AS Wendy walked with modest grace between the desks. Even Jack Culverhouse was applauding.

'Didn't have you down as a clapper, guv,' Wendy said.

'I'm not, but it's been a long time since I've seen a pair of legs and an arse like that.'

'Hospital food. Enough to make anyone lose three stone.'

'I'll bear that in mind next time my brother is strangling the shit out of me. Every cloud, eh?'

Wendy managed a wry laugh. She could either laugh or cry and she had done enough of one of those over the past few weeks.

'Well, welcome back. I think it's safe to say we probably won't see the likes of a case like that for a while.'

'We definitely won't,' Wendy said. 'I don't have any other brothers left.'

Culverhouse matched her wry laugh of relief.

'Tell me, Knight. For my own peace of mind. Did you really not have even the slightest inkling that Michael was involved?'

'No, how could I?'

'Heh. Bloody good job I put PC Baxter's name forward for a fast-track promotion instead of yours then, isn't it?' Culverhouse replied.

'You did *what*?'

'Well, are you surprised? Four bloody weeks off work doesn't quite cut the mustard either, does it? Back in my day, I'd've been back at work by eight the next morning. Now sit down. You've got some paperwork to catch up on.'

Wendy had the feeling that some things were just never destined to change.

Get more of my books FREE!

Thank you for reading Too Close For Comfort. I hope it was as much fun for you as it was for me writing it.

To say thank you, I'd like to give you some of my books and short stories for FREE. Read on to get yours…

If you enjoyed the book, please do leave a review on Amazon. Reviews mean an awful lot to writers and they help us to find new readers more than almost anything else. It would be very much appreciated.

I love hearing from my readers, too, so please do feel free to get in touch with me. You can contact me via my website, on Twitter @adamcroft and you can 'like' my Facebook page at http://www.facebook.com/adamcroftbooks.

Last of all, but certainly not least, I'd like to let you know that members of my email club have access to FREE, exclusive books and short stories which aren't available anywhere else. There's a whole lot more, too, so please join the club (for free!) at adamcroft.net/email-club

For more information, visit my website: adamcroft.net

ACKNOWLEDGEMENTS

My unwavering thanks go to the following people, without whom The Thirteenth Room would not have been possible:

Helen Armitage for the extensive information on pathology proceedings and the inner workings of the coroner's court.

Simon Clarke for his number crunching and statistical analysis of suicide rates, murder rates and combining these with statistics on handedness.

David Parry, former Detective Sergeant with Leicestershire Police for his insight and information on police procedures surrounding suspected suicides.

Kate Jones and Charlotte Knowles of the Down's Syndrome Association for spending the time with me to explain more about antenatal screening processes and helping ensure accuracy.

Joanne, Manuela and Jonathan, my editors and beta readers who make sure the book is actually readable.

Debbie for the superb cover design.

Amanda Ashton at Blush Book Design for the fantastic typesetting and formatting.

My wife for her unwavering patience in fixing my plot holes and generally putting the icing on the very rough and unbaked cakes which are my initial drafts and ideas.

Everyone who has asked when my next book will be out and emailed or otherwise contacted me to say how much they love the series. It's your support and love for the books which spurs me on to write more (and faster).

And finally, Mother Nature for ensuring the weather has been too unpleasant for me to want to sit in a pub garden and instead keeping me at my laptop over the winter.

Knight & Culverhouse return in

GUILTY AS SIN

OUT NOW

When seventeen-year-old Danielle Levy goes missing one lunchtime, DS Wendy Knight and DCI Jack Culverhouse believe they have a routine case on their hands.

When a prominent local businessman is found dead in his warehouse, however, the case takes a whole new disturbing turn as Knight and Culverhouse begin to unravel the connections between the two cases which lead to a dark and disturbing secret.

Turn the page to read the first chapter...

GUILTY AS SIN

CHAPTER 1

It was the last day of Danielle Levy's life.

As she sauntered round the corner into Heathcote Road on her way back from a hard half-day's work at sixth-form college, she was glad that it hadn't been a full day and that she could enjoy the afternoon in the sun.

It had been Maths today. It was always bloody Maths. Despite the fact that she had chosen to study Drama and

English Literature as her two main A-levels, her mother had insisted that she choose at least one 'proper' subject. She'd thrown in Classics as her fourth option. Another protest to piss her parents off, but she was actually quite enjoying it. She hoped one day to be a Drama teacher, or perhaps English. She'd be one of those cool teachers that all the kids loved, not like those stuffy idiots at Woodlands.

Woodlands was all right, she supposed. It wasn't an all-purpose college like the one she had planned to attend before her family moved to Mildenheath, but it was all right. The sixth-form college was somewhat amalgamated with the upper school, which ruined the sense of adult independence as far as she was concerned. How could you feel like you were no longer at school when you were in a school? The same teachers, the same classrooms. The same snotty-nosed little brats who didn't know what it meant to be grown up. She'd have to deal with that when she was a teacher, but she'd find a way.

Every day when she turned the corner into Heathcote Road, her heart sank a little. True enough, it was the road she lived on, but her house was a good seven hundred yards further along the road; a road which seemed to get longer and longer every time she walked it. She had lived at 101 Heathcote Road only for a couple of months, but she had already become attached to the house. It was on a quiet estate on the edge of town, mostly three- and four-bedroom houses, nice spacious gardens and no problems to worry about. Not like the last house. Passing the parade of shops, walking up the hill and exiting the right-hand bend to see her house standing proud in the summer sunshine always made her feel warm and glorious. It was home.

Darren's van was park jauntily on the cracked concrete driveway as she skirted around the edge of the lawn towards the front door. Her step-father tended to finish work early on Fridays. Not that he didn't finish early on every other day. She guessed there wasn't much call for carpet fitters after 2pm on a weekday.

Turning her key in the lock and crunching the bottom of the door over the pile of letters which lay in wait on the doormat, she heaved her rucksack against the wine rack, picked up the post and made her way towards the kitchen. The door had been locked, so it was clear to Danielle that she was alone in the house. No biggie, though. It was a Friday and Darren often brought his van home and went straight to the pub after work on Fridays. A few hours of afternoon sun in the beer garden. Who could blame him?

It was then that she heard the familiar creaking of the back door.

For more information, visit my website: adamcroft.net

Fancy something cosy?

Exit Stage Left
(Kempston Hardwick Mystery #1)

Charlie Sparks had it all. A former primetime television personality, his outdated style has seen him relegated to the scrapheap.

When he collapses and dies during a stand-up routine at a local pub, mysterious bystander Kempston Hardwick is compelled to investigate his suspicious death.

As Hardwick begins to unravel the mystery, he quickly comes to realise that Charlie Sparks's death throws up more peculiar questions than answers.

For more information, visit my website: adamcroft.net

Made in the USA
Columbia, SC
26 February 2018